"Is it my imagination," Josh said, "or is something clicking here between us?"

"Clicking is not the right word," Juliet said. Blooming, maybe. She looked at his mouth, and could not even remember when she had so longed for a kiss. "It isn't your imagination," she said, and swallowed.

"That's what I thought," he said, the voice rumbling out of that deep chest with the depth of a drum. His nostrils flared as he looked at her mouth, at her breasts, back to her face. "Probably shouldn't do anything about it, though."

Honestly, what was this? This narcotic spell he cast? Would he kiss her? Would she let him?

"I can be strong, princess," he said, "but not if you keep looking at me like that."

Dear Reader,

The leaves aren't the only things changing colors this October. Starting this month, you'll notice Silhouette Intimate Moments is evolving into its vibrant new look, and that's just the start of some exciting changes we're undergoing. As of February 2007, we will have a new name, Silhouette Romantic Suspense. Not to worry, these are still the breathtaking romances—don't forget the suspense!—that you've come to know and love in Intimate Moments. Keep your eyes open for our new look over the next few months as we transition fully to our new appearance. As always, we deliver on our promise of romance, danger and excitement.

Speaking of romance, danger and excitement, award-winning author Ruth Wind brings us *Juliet's Law* (#1435), the debut of her miniseries SISTERS OF THE MOUNTAIN. An attorney must depend on a handsome tribal officer to prove her sister's innocence on murder charges. Wendy Rosnau continues her arresting SPY GAMES series with *Undercover Nightingale* (#1436) in which an explosives expert falls for an undercover agent and learns just how deceiving looks can be.

You'll nearly swoon as a Navajo investigator protects a traumatized photojournalist in *The Last Warrior* (#1437) by Kylie Brant. Don't miss Loreth Anne White's new miniseries, SHADOW SOLDIERS, and its first story, *The Heart of a Mercenary* (#1438), a gripping tale with a to-die-for alpha hero!

This month, and every month, let our stories sweep you into an exciting world of passion and suspense. Happy reading!

Sincerely,

Patience Smith
Associate Senior Editor

Silhouette®

INTIMATE MOMENTS™

Published by Silhouette Books

America's Publisher of Contemporary Romance

ISBN-13: 978-0-373-27505-2
ISBN-10: 0-373-27505-6

JULIET'S LAW

This edition published by arrangement with Harlequin Books S.A.

Visit Silhouette Books at www.eHarlequin.com

Printed in U.S.A.

Books by Ruth Wind

Silhouette Intimate Moments

Breaking the Rules #587
**Reckless* #796
**Her Ideal Man* #801
For Christmas, Forever #898
†*Rio Grande Wedding* #964
**Beautiful Stranger* #1011
Born Brave #1106
‡*Juliet's Law* #1435

Silhouette Bombshell

Countdown #36
The Diamond Secret #83

Silhouette Special Edition

Strangers on a Train #555
Summer's Freedom #588
Light of Day #635
A Minute To Smile #742
Jezebel's Blues #785
Walk in Beauty #881
The Last Chance Ranch #977
Rainsinger #1031
**Marriage Material* #1108
†*Meant To Be Married* #1194

*The Last Roundup
†Men of the Land
‡Sisters of the Mountain

RUTH WIND

is the award-winning author of both contemporary and historical romance novels. She lives in the mountains of the Southwest with her two growing sons and many animals in a hundred-year-old house the town blacksmith built. The only hobby she has had since she started writing is tending the ancient garden of irises, lilies and lavender beyond her office window, and she says she can think of no more satisfying way to spend a life than growing children, books and flowers. Ruth Wind also writes women's fiction under the name Barbara Samuel. You can visit her Web site at www.barbarasamuel.com.

For Madi Nance.
Remember, you are a princess,
and princesses can do anything they set their minds to.

Prologue

"Juliet," said her sister Desdemona over the phone, "I'm in trouble. Real trouble."

Juliet, scrunched in a TV-watching coma on the couch, cleared her throat. "Yeah?" Desi's voice had been so bland Juliet didn't immediately see any reason to get excited. Or sit up for that matter. She chose an M&M out of the bowl in her lap. "What's wrong?"

"I have a shotgun in my lap," she said distinctly, "and I need you to tell me why I shouldn't shoot my lying pig of a husband when he comes through our front door."

Juliet sat up. M&M's scattered across the bare wooden floor, because until that minute, she'd been eating the candy and watching her new favorite soap opera. It was important, she had decided, to eat the candy in order of color: first brown, because they were so boring, then yellow, because that was close to brown, then green for grass, then red.

In order to keep herself from eating an entire king-sized bag in five minutes flat, she'd also made some rules about how to eat them, once they were sorted into colors. She could only put one in her mouth at a time, and she wasn't allowed to bite them—only suck the candy coating from the chocolate, then let the chocolate melt in her mouth. If she followed the rule, the bag would last through both *The Guiding Light* and *Days of Our Lives,* and then it was time for lunch.

Juliet liked structure. Since she'd been asked to take a leave of absence from her Los Angeles firm, there was no real structure to her life at the moment. She made do with what she could get—candy rituals, reliable television programs, meal times.

But this—! A crisis was even better than structure. In a crisis, there were steps to follow, a plan to make, a defined course of action. In this crisis, for example, she knew exactly what to do first. She put the bowl to one side and brushed blue M&M's off her lap.

"Desi?" she said gently. "You have a gun?"

"Of course I have a gun! I live in the wilds of the Colorado Rockies." She sniffed, the kind of thick-sounding snort that came after serious crying. "There are mountain lions up here."

"But you're holding it now? The gun?"

"Yes." Her sister now started to sob at the other end of the phone, that desperate, end-of-my-rope kind of crying Juliet had heard too often as a volunteer at a community center for immigrant women in L.A.

"Yes," Desi repeated. "He's out with his mistress and he knows I know it and I've told him to get out of my house and go get a divorce, but he won't do it, because he won't give up his half of the land, and I don't know what to do!"

"Desi," Juliet said, making her voice both smooth and authoritative, "take the bullets out of the shotgun and throw them out the window."

"He deserves to get shot," she insisted.

"No doubt," Juliet agreed, "but if you kill him, you'll go to jail. And that would be a very bad thing for you. Do you hear me?"

A sob came through the phone. "Who would convict me? A lying, cheating scumbag who will not move out of my house and instead is torturing me like this? This has been going on for three months! He deserves it!"

"Yes," Juliet said again. "Desi, please, sweetie, take the bullets out of the gun and go throw them out the window."

"They're not technically bullets."

"Whatever you call them, sis. Get rid of them."

There was a little rattle on the line, the sound of the receiver being put down. In the background, Juliet heard a clank, and Desi came back on. "Okay," she said in a raw voice. "I threw the shells out the window."

Juliet let go of her breath. "Good. Very good." She knew the very next thing to do, too. "I'll be there tomorrow, okay? Don't do *anything* until then. Promise me?"

Desi's voice was small. "Okay."

"Think of your wolves. Who will take care of them if you go to jail?"

A long quiet burned down the wire. "You're right," Desi said at last, and there was another kind of brokenness to it. "Please come, Juliet. I really need you."

"I'm on my way, sis."

Chapter 1

The skies were heavy over the mountains of Mariposa when Josh Mad Calf fastened his daughter into her car seat in the half-back bench of his massive pickup truck. The four-year-old wore a blue knitted hat on her glossy dark head, and her eyes had the glazed blankness of mid-afternoon. "Sleepy, kiddo?"

"Don't call me that!" she said, glaring at him.

He chuckled and touched her nose. "Okay, rabbit."

"Not that, either!"

"Okay, wolf-girl."

"Dad-DEE!" she complained.

"Sorry," he said, grinning, and tucked a few bags of groceries around her feet—a handful of supplies for himself and his friend Desi, just in case the threatening snow turned into a blizzard. As he slammed the door firmly, he narrowed his eyes and looked up. Burly blue mountains surrounded the town, and clouds had moved halfway down their sides, hiding the entire line of ridges and most of the still-bare ski runs.

They wouldn't be bare long. A few cottony bits of snow were spitting out of the sky, but it would be a few hours until the heart of the storm moved in. By then he and Glory would be tucked into their snug house, a fire roaring in the potbellied stove, soup bubbling on the stove for their supper, a dog snoring on the hearth.

A good life. Good enough. In the old days, he'd imagined a woman for himself in that picture—a mother for Glory—but that had turned out badly. Very badly. As he headed away from town on narrow roads, he remembered to be grateful. Grateful for simple things like his daughter safe in his care, knowing she'd be fed well tonight and sleep in a clean, warm bed.

It hadn't always been that way. He looked in the rearview mirror and saw that she'd fallen asleep. Her cheeks were rosy, her dark eyelashes a half oval. He could never get over the fragility of her closed eyelids, the sweetness of her perfect skin, her tiny fingernails.

Several miles into the mountains, he turned off on an even narrower road, this one dirt, and bumpy. It looped around wooded landscapes alongside a stream, and opened finally into a pristine meadow, with spectacular views of the high, craggy peaks of the San Juan Mountains. Well, there was a view on clear days, anyway. This afternoon, only the blue lower skirts showed beneath blouses of thick clouds.

A collection of low outbuildings spread out to the east of the meadow. In the center was a small, neat house built of pine. Smoke came out of the chimney. Josh smiled to himself as he followed the driveway around to the front of the house. Desi would have the kettle on. Maybe he'd have a cup of coffee before heading home. She'd been going through a rough time.

As he rounded her house, his smile faded. A grim tableau was playing out in front of the little house. Desi, a tall sturdy woman with a glossy black braid, was standing on her back steps, a rifle in her hand. Her expression was grim.

The rifle was pointed at Claude Tsosie, Desi's soon-to-be-ex-husband, who also sported a long black braid. He wore a jean jacket and boots, and silver jewelry on his wrists. Josh shook his head. He'd never really liked Claude, an artist who lived too much on his talent and never spoke the truth if there was a way around it, but he didn't especially want to see him dead.

A third, unexpected player was a fragile-looking blond woman who stood by her car, frightened and obviously unsure of what to do. Her boots were the city sort—not high-heeled, especially, or pointed, but square and polished. Wouldn't be worth a damn in the snow that was coming. She looked over at Josh's truck, entreaty on her—he saw now—very pretty face.

From the glove box, Josh took his badge. He was a tribal policeman and technically had no jurisdiction off the reservation, but Claude wouldn't pay much attention.

He glanced over his shoulder to see that Glory was still sound asleep, and climbed quietly out of the truck.

* * *

Juliet stood frozen by her rental car, praying that Desi would not actually kill her husband. At the moment, the decision seemed to rest on Claude, who had by turns been cajoling Desi, then turning toward Juliet.

"Sister," he said in his reedy, sexy voice, his hands spread out in appeal, "can't you talk some sense into her? I just want to get a few of my things, and then I'm gone."

From the porch, Desi said, "Don't try to drag her into this. Get into your truck and drive out of here before I shoot you."

Juliet, once very good in a crisis, wrapped her arms around her ribs and tried desperately to remember how her old self would have handled this scene. She couldn't remember. Sometimes lately, it seemed there was a sinkhole in the center of her life, and all sorts of things were falling into it. Memories. Jobs. Maybe her fiancé.

How to handle a crisis.

So, when the big black truck pulled into the drive, Juliet was relieved. She wouldn't have to keep Desi from shooting Claude, or keep Claude from trying to take things that were not technically his. Juliet clasped her thin coat closer to herself—Southern California did not require the kind of coats you needed in Colorado—and gave the person in the truck an urgent expression: *help!*

In a moment, the door opened and a man climbed down and closed his door with odd gentleness.

Juliet blinked. He was obviously Native American, with hair the color of ink tumbling in a straight heavy gloss down his back. Tall, square-shouldered and lean, he wore a sheepskin jacket and jeans and had long, capable-looking hands.

But it was his face that captured her. Eyes as large and dark as a deer's, with a generous mouth to balance cheekbones as severe as a cliff. Not beautiful. Not even handsome, particularly.

Definitely compelling.

Especially now, as he advanced toward Desi and Claude. It was as if an aura came with him, a force field. Juliet wished—suddenly and fiercely—that she had learned that trick.

He moved without hurry across the yard. As he approached, he said, "Claude," and his voice rumbled out of his chest, as if a grizzly bear was doing the talking. The sound was low and full, an umbrella of protective sound. "You know you aren't supposed to be here."

"I just want to get my stuff," Claude responded.

"Get out of here," Desi said in a raw voice. Her face was blotchy with tears or anger or both. She raised the rifle to her shoulder. "Get. Out."

Claude raised his hands. "Take it easy."

From somewhere to the east came a howl, long and chilling, and then another and another—Desi's wolves, crying out from their sanctuary, as if they knew what was transpiring. The wolves were her special project, rescued from every imaginable situation, and the sound of their howls was chilling and primitive.

No one moved.

And then, as if the sky had been ripped open with a knife, it started to snow. Juliet looked up in amazement at gigantic flakes, as big and thick as slices of white bread, tumbling out of the sky. They stuck to the three dark heads to make lacy caps, and with that odd sense of disconnect that had plagued her so much lately, Juliet lost interest in her sister and the scene, and held out a hand to catch a snowflake. They touched her palm and melted white to silver. Pristine. Unspoiled.

The stranger's voice brought her attention back to the scene. "Desi, please put down the rifle. We all love you and need you and this is not the answer."

"Tell him to get off my land and I'll put down the rifle."

"It's not just your land!" Claude protested, taking a step forward.

Desi fired, striking the dirt by Claude's foot. He yelped and jumped backward, "All right. I'm leaving. Crazy—"

Desi calmly took another bullet out of her pocket and began to reload.

Claude climbed into his three-quarter-ton pickup truck, a vehicle even Juliet could recognize as fully loaded. The engine sounded like a semi as he fired it up and backed away. He rolled his window down. "Desi, babe," he said, one last attempt. "Can't we—"

"Don't *ever* talk to me again," Desi said.

The other man, the Indian, banged the flat of his hand on the truck, as if urging a dog or a horse to get along down the road. "Move on, Claude. It's done for today."

And, finally, Claude pulled away, his truck roaring down the dirt road. Not even gravel this far out, Juliet had discovered to her dismay. By midwinter, it would be practically impassable.

The stranger approached Desi, who stood on the porch with a blank expression on her face, and plucked the rifle out of her hand. With an expert gesture, he cracked open the barrel and emptied it. "I hate to leave you out here without protection, Desi," he said in that rumbling voice, "but I hate more to see you kill him, and end up in jail."

"You can't take my gun, Josh," Desi said. "I promise I won't kill him."

Josh kept on with his task.

At last Desi seemed to realize Juliet was there, and gave her sister a wan smile. "Hi, baby," she said.

The stillness broke around Juliet. She dashed across the yard and flung her arms around her big sister. "I'm here now," Juliet said. "We have each other."

And in a most un-big-sisterlike way, Desi broke down, tears streaming out of her eyes as she clung to Juliet. "Thank you. I'm sorry, I love you, I wish I could be stronger for you right now, but I'm just falling apart."

The man put his hand on Juliet's shoulder, and she startled violently, breaking away from her sister's hug, and backing away in a most inelegant way. Her left eye started that weird twitching thing it kept doing lately.

"Let's get her inside," the man said, appearing not to notice. "In case Claude gets mad and comes back."

Juliet nodded jerkily. She was oddly aware of the back of her neck, of the top of her head, parts of herself she never noticed. She looked at his shoes. They were sturdy, steel-toed boots. Serious and stable. He wore jeans that were just tight enough to show his lean, muscular thighs, and a sheepskin jacket that had been worn a few seasons. He smelled of leather and morning, an oddly compelling combination, and she wanted to lean closer, take that scent more deeply into her lungs. She swayed, dizzy from travel or danger or him.

He looked at her closely. "Are you okay?"

Fiancé, she told herself. Remember Scott. She nodded, a little too enthusiastically. "Fine."

"That was a tough scene to run into."

She nodded, lifted a shoulder. "I really am okay." Fear wasn't the problem these days, except the weird twitch and that exaggerated startle reflex. It was more this sense of not being able to really connect to anything that was driving her crazy.

The man said, "My daughter's asleep in the truck. Will you keep an eye on her until I take your sister inside?"

"Sure, of course." She pointed a thumb over her shoulder. "You want me to go stand there?"

But he'd already gone inside, nudging Desi along. Juliet stood on the porch and looked at the big truck, disappearing now under a thin covering of snow. It looked fake, as if someone sprinkled it out of some big box overhead, clumps falling out every so often to land with a puffy splash on the hood. She tugged her sleeves down over her hands and went to stand by the truck.

As if marauders might be coming to fling open the door and steal the little girl away.

Now that the drama had died down, the air was utterly, completely still. It almost held a sense of tension, as if the air were waiting for something. A gunshot? A cry?

No, none of those. Using a trick one of her therapists taught her, she pushed the dark thoughts away and willfully reached for good ones. The silence was waiting for what *good* thing? Laughter. Happiness. A bluebird.

She snorted to herself. Yeah, right. A little bluebird of happiness right here in the falling snow.

The man came out of the house, and she thought again what a sharp, strong face he had. A ripple of nervousness—or maybe attraction?—moved through her. His hair, straight and thick, was so black it sucked light into it. "Hello," he said, "I'm Josh Mad Calf."

"Metcalf?"

He grinned. His eyes crinkled gorgeously at the corners, sending a fan of sun lines into his dark cheeks. "Mad Calf," he repeated, enunciating carefully.

"Thanks for saving the day."

"All in a day's work, ma'am," he said, and winked. "I'm just going to get my daughter from the truck. Why don't you go in and keep your sister company?"

"Right. Yes. Good idea."

In the kitchen, Juliet put the kettle on the tiny, two-burner stove and turned on the fire beneath it, bemused by the bright blue flame that burst to life with a little pop. She had an electric stove at home. Gas seemed old-fashioned, though her friend the chef swore it was the only possible heating element for a serious cook.

Not that Desi—or Juliet for that matter—would ever qualify. Both had been too busy to learn to cook, really. And it wasn't as if their mother was the sort to have taught them. If Carol Rousseau had ever in her life cooked anything more complicated than a cup of tea, Juliet would be very surprised.

With the water on to boil, Juliet looked around to see what had changed since her last visit. The cabin was small, only two rooms; the kitchen/living area, and the sleeping area, with a bed and a futon and desk, plus the postage-stamp-sized bathroom. There was a very small generator for electricity, and the stove ran on propane. Two potbellied stoves, one in each room, provided heat.

Primitive, but not as primitive as it had been. At least there was a toilet and a tub now—things that had been missing the first couple of times Juliet had come to visit. Desi and Claude had built the cabin themselves, a little at a time, and the plan—at least until the marriage had started falling apart—had been to add a room every year.

Juliet found visiting fun for a week or two, but it got old to have to be so careful with everything she used so casually in the city, things a person took for granted. Water, electricity, heat. Desi didn't take long hot baths, as Juliet did in her old Hollywood condo, or leave the water running when she brushed her teeth, or play the television for company. Desi didn't actually own a television—she said they used too much power, and without a dish, there wasn't much reception anyway.

Despite the rustic aspect, the cabin was quite charming, with thick, western-themed blankets on the bed and futon, and a potbellied stove burning wood to warm the room. The windows framed views that were breathtaking on a clear day, and even now, the snow falling on long-needled ponderosa pines looked serene and inviting. As if to complete the picture, a huge dog with a thick, silvery coat wandered in through a dog door in the back, and came over to sniff Juliet's knee.

"Hey, Tecumseh," Juliet said, and bent down to rub his thick fur. "Long time no see."

He lifted his chin to let his chest be scrubbed, then wandered over to slump down by the fire. Desi was in the bathroom, and when she didn't come out fairly soon, Juliet went to the door and knocked gently. "Hey, sis, are you all right?"

"No," she said, the word muffled by tears or a towel or maybe both. "But I'll be out in a minute, okay?"

"I'm just going to go get my suitcase."

"Fine."

Juliet didn't move. She stood there, forehead against the door, and wondered what to do. Desi didn't make a habit of emotional scenes; in fact, of the three Rousseau sisters, Desi had always been the sensible, practical one. Juliet was the good girl. Miranda was the artist, the drama queen. Desi had always been the levelheaded person in any group, the scientist and practical one; picking up the pieces for other people, helping them put their problems into perspective. Desi got done what needed to be done.

One of the reasons, come to think of it, that it was a good thing someone had taken the gun away from her. If Desi was so despairing that she had loaded a shotgun and aimed it at her ex, if she was so overwhelmed that she was weeping in the bathroom, things were really dire.

Just this once, Juliet could be the rescuer in the family. "Josh will be back in a minute, too," she said through the door. "Wash your face and come out when you're ready."

Outside, Juliet was surprised by the density of snow. It already clustered on the steps like down feathers, so light the flakes scattered in front of her feet as she walked toward her car. Josh approached, carrying a car seat with a very, very conked-out little girl in it. Juliet smiled and went for her bag, and carried it back inside right behind him.

Just as Josh was settling the car seat down, the kettle started to whistle—loudly—and Juliet dashed into the kitchen area to pull it off the stove. She poured hot water into a fat yellow ceramic teapot she'd already primed. "Nothing like tea to cure what ails you," she said half to the man, half to herself.

"So my granny says," Josh said.

"Mine, too." She held out her hand. "I'm Juliet, by the way. Desi's younger sister."

Josh reached for her hand. His was a giant paw, the palm as big as her whole hand, and he raised his left, too, making a sandwich that covering hers completely. "Good to meet you."

"Not *that* much younger," Desi said, coming out of the bathroom. Her nose was red and her eyes were swollen, but she looked more like herself. "She's the middle child."

Josh looked over his shoulder, but didn't let go. As gingerly as possible, Juliet tugged her hand out of his grip.

He didn't seem to mind. "Sisters always fight about that," he said in a jovial tone. Juliet liked him for trying to create a sense of normality after the intense scene outside.

"Are you okay?" Juliet asked her sister.

Desi swiped hair off her face. "I'll live." She hugged Josh, and leaned into his chest. "Thank you."

He hugged her back, and in his bearish embrace, tall, square Desi looked tiny. Their mother had always called Desi an Amazon, and not in a nice way. It came out in sentences like, "You are such an Amazon you could never wear those shoes," or, "Will you try to stop clumping around like an Amazon, Desdemona?"

So mean, Juliet thought now, feeling a surge of fierce love for her sister. Their mother had been highly critical of all of them, but Juliet privately thought Desi had got the worst of it.

Lifting the lid on the teapot, she said, "I think it's ready now. Who wants tea?"

"Me, me, me." Desi sat down heavily at the round wooden table. "There are some oatmeal cookies in that jar over there, too, if you want to put a pile of them out for us."

Josh sat down next to her, rubbing his hands. "Oatmeal. All right!"

For all his size, Juliet thought he moved with a surprising grace, as light on his feet as a deer. She put the cookies down in front of him.

"Thanks," he said, and raised his eyes to look at her straight on. For a moment, Juliet didn't think to look away; and it was the *oddest* sensation: she felt as if she plunged into a vat of warm chocolate, seeing there in the long-lashed eyes a spirit of gentleness, beauty, something still and kind.

With a man like this at your back, nothing too

terrible could happen. She wondered where his wife was. There was no ring on his finger, but that didn't always mean anything.

Realizing that she stared, Juliet looked away, poured tea for Desi, and passed her a crystal bowl, stacked neatly with sugar cubes and a little pair of tongs. It had belonged to their grandmother, an east-coast blue blood; Daughters of the American Revolution, roots back to the Pilgrims. As she passed it, Juliet thought of long, quiet afternoons in the Maine "cottage," spent curled up in window seats, with the wind whipping the sea into a frenzy beyond, tea served late in the afternoon with tiny spoons and pots of cream and little cookies. It was a surprisingly rich memory. "So glad you have this bowl," Juliet said.

Desi nodded.

"Are you the artist sister or the lawyer?" Josh asked.

"Lawyer. Sort of." She flipped her shoulder against the thudding wound she sometimes felt over losing that, too, her job as a civil rights lawyer. Not fair. Not *fair!* "I'm taking some time off."

He picked up his tea. Blew on it. For one blistering moment, Juliet wondered if he knew her story, if Desi had told him. Her ears felt hot with embarrassment.

But of course Desi wouldn't tell Juliet's secrets.

Josh said, "It was nice of you to take time off to take care of your sister. She needs you."

"I do," Desi said, touching Juliet's hand.

"I'm glad to be here."

In the corner, the little girl in the car seat suddenly stirred. She kicked her feet, lifted her head, and peered at the adults in confusion. "Hi, Auntie Dez," she said. "Am I staying here?"

"Not this time, sweetheart. But I do have a cookie if you want to come get one."

"You got cookies?" The girl pushed out of her coat, discarded it in the middle of the floor. "What kind?"

"Glory," her father said, "What do we do with our coats?"

The child sighed, dropped her shoulders in exaggerated put-upon-ness, and clomped back to the coat. With rolling eyes, she picked it up and put it on the couch. She had a black braid that reached her hips, big dark eyes, and very rosy brown cheeks. She looked exactly like the kewpie Indian dolls they used to sell in tourist shops around here. Juliet wondered, suddenly, if such things were still sold.

Glory clomped back toward the table. Only when she rounded the corner of the counter did she catch sight of Juliet. The girl stopped dead, staring, her little mouth open in surprise.

"Hi," Juliet said.

The little girl still said nothing. She just gaped. After a few seconds, she frowned and her hand flew to her cheeks in what would be a mocking expression in an adult but was simply the most natural expression of surprise and shock a four-year-old could muster.

"Oh!" she said, as if she'd just figured it out. Her voice was breathy with awe. "You're the *princess,* aren't you?"

Chapter 2

Juliet wasn't sure how to respond.

"The princess?" she echoed, trying to figure out what Glory meant. "Am I?" She glanced at Josh, raised her eyebrows in question.

He gave her a bewildered shrug. He didn't know, either.

Glory came forward, her eyes fixed on Juliet. She leaned on her father's knee, coquettishly flirting with both Juliet and her father. "Can I sit by her? The princess?"

"If she doesn't mind, that's fine."

"Of course I don't mind." Juliet moved over a little to make room, glancing up at her sister.

Despite her weariness, Desi gave a wan grin. "As a rule, she's not crazy about strangers."

"At all," Josh added.

Glory, oddly self-possessed, came around the table. With her hands folded in front of her, she said formally, with enunciation quite clear on each "t," "Is it all right if I sit here, Princess?"

"Yes," Juliet said, and patted the chair. "Please do."

The little girl sat down and spread a napkin over her lap. To the other adults, she announced, "The princess and I are having cookies."

"I see that." Desi blinked, and Juliet saw that she was very near tears again. Of all the things in the world she'd wanted a child most of all. She and Claude had been planning to adopt....

Juliet felt pierced, too, for reasons she couldn't pinpoint. There was something so innocent, almost magical, about the little girl's belief.

"They're very good cookies, aren't they?" Juliet said.

"My grandma makes better ones."

"This is your grandma's recipe, silly girl." Desi said, and gave her one. "I even put in the ginger."

"Listen," Josh said. "I don't want to interrupt, but we need to get some things ironed out here. Let me ask some questions of a purely practical nature."

Desi sipped her tea. Blinked hard. Nodded.

"Do you have a restraining order?"

"No. Not yet. I guess I was hoping I wouldn't have to do that. We've been together for fifteen years—I thought I knew him better than this."

"Princess," Glory said. "You aren't eating."

"You're right." Juliet picked up a cookie. It held absolutely no appeal, but she nibbled an edge anyway. She would have to get out her supply of M&M's. A girl had to eat, after all. Something about the small, bite-sizedness of the candies appealed to her these days. M&M's, pistachio nuts in their shells, croutons, baby carrots—she lived on them. They also required no attention when one ate them while reading—a big plus. Food for the belly, food for the mind. Presto! Two jobs at once.

When in Rome, however, one did what the Romans did. She bit into the cookie and chewed as well as she could. "Desi, you need to get the paperwork done. You *have* filed for divorce, right?"

Desi examined her cookie, plucked out a raisin. "Not exactly. I guess I just kept thinking this was all going to be a bad dream."

"Time to wake up." Juliet had seen too many cases like this go awry, for all kinds of reasons. "I really don't want to see you lose the land."

"I know."

"I'll go with you," Juliet said. "I'll help you. We'll go to town tomorrow and take care of it, all right?"

Desi nodded. "Okay. Tomorrow."

"Princess," Glory said, touching her hand. "If you came to town, I could show you my shoes!"

"Shoes?" Juliet grinned. "Do you have a lot of shoes?"

"No," she said matter-of-factly. "But I have some red ones." She leaned in close and covered her mouth, whispering, "They have diamonds on them!"

"Wow. I can't wait." Caught in the moment, she bent and whispered, "I *love* red shoes."

"You do? Do you have some?"

"Not with me," Juliet said.

"Where are they?"

"I left them at home. At my home in California."

Glory's eyes widened. "Do you live by Disneyland? You can see Sleeping Beauty and Cinderella at Disneyland, you know."

As it happened—"I do live by Disneyland, actually. You will have to come see me and we'll go together."

"*That* would be good!" Glory looked at her father. "Daddy, do you think we could do that sometime, maybe?"

"We'll see, kiddo." Josh chuckled. To Juliet he said, "You've been anointed."

"Daddy," Glory said, "don't talk to her right now. She needs to eat." With great tenderness, she patted Juliet's hand. "Eat, Princess, I'll watch out for you."

The simple faith in the little girl's face was almost more than Juliet could bear. Sucking in a steadying breath, she bent down and patted the child's hand. "Thank you, sweetie."

Joshua Mad Calf was not a romantic kind of guy. He liked vigorous things, *manly* things like football and race cars and big trucks splashing through the mud. He tended toward the practical, and his job as a cop, as well as his history, had taught him that life was not sweet or nice or fair. In terms of women, he tended to go for a peasant type—strong and curvy, a woman who could work the land, take care of children, cook for twenty at the drop of a hat.

And yet, just like his daughter, he was enchanted by Juliet. He tried to avoid staring, but rarely had seen a woman so pretty. Not *beautiful,* which was too much, too intimidating, too much trouble. Not *attractive,* which was too sedate. Not even cute, which didn't bring enough weight to it.

Juliet was *pretty,* like a pink and white winter morning. Smooth, delicate skin, the softness of pale blond hair tumbling in waves over her slim shoulders, china-blue eyes. She looked exactly like the drawing of a princess in a storybook, right down to the red bow of mouth.

And like a princess under threat of a dragon, there was a vulnerable and fragile air about her. He hadn't missed the exchange of glances between the sisters, the unspoken communication that flowed between them. There was something going on here.

They were finishing their tea and Josh was thinking, reluctantly, that they'd have to take their leave when Glory said, "Auntie, can we feed the wolves?"

"They were already fed today, sweetheart, but we can go see them if your dad doesn't mind."

"Can we, Daddy?"

"You betcha."

It pierced him when Glory reached out and put her small brown hand over Juliet's pale white one, and lifted her guileless face. "Do you want to come, Princess?"

And what, he wondered, was that about, anyway? To say Glory didn't like strangers was like saying the *Titanic* was a big boat. It took months for her to thaw around a new adult, though she was fine with other children. What was it about Juliet that made Glory think she was a princess?

"Yes, very much." Her voice held much more weight

than you'd expect. It was strong and dulcet, well-modulated. He supposed that was at least partly from being in the courtroom, but it lent an oddly royal air.

Get a grip, he told himself. "C'mon, kiddo. Let's put your coat back on if we're going outside."

"I want Princess to do it," she said, throwing her arm around her body so he couldn't slip the coat on.

"If you're rude, we'll go home," he said. Quietly.

She flicked a glance toward him, perhaps gauging how serious he was. Something she saw convinced her he meant it. Lowering her arm, she said, "Princess, will you help me put on my coat? Please?"

Juliet looked up at him for permission. Something about the angle or the light made her pupils nearly disappear, which made her eyes look as if they were made of glass, like a doll.

Fragile, girlish. Not his type at all.

And yet, he kept noticing other things, too. There was nothing girlish about her breasts, full and bouncy beneath her sweater, or her mouth, which, despite the princess bow, was full and red, as sensual a mouth as he'd ever seen, or the roundness of her bottom in her jeans. The Rousseau sisters would never make the fashion runway, but he was glad there were still women in the world with some curves to them.

Down boy, he thought with some amusement, but still found himself taking one last look from the corner of his eye. Discreetly. Plump flesh beneath a thin purple sweater. Nice. Definitely nice.

Enough. Handing Glory's coat to her, he said, "Go ahead."

He turned away. There was no room in his life for a woman, and he had to be wary because of Glory, anyway. To make up for the nightmare eight months she'd spent with her mother, the little girl needed absolute stability, and no possibility of loss.

"Ready?" Desi said, tugging her long hair from beneath her coat. The dog got up and wagged his tail. She opened the door to let him go out.

They all traipsed outside in a line, Tecumseh the white wolf-Akita mix, then Desi leading with her strong walk, then Juliet and Glory, holding hands, and Josh in the rear. Snow still fell in heavy drifts, and he thought it was time they should get home.

First the wolves, then home for supper with his little girl.

Away from the sweet temptation of the princess.

Juliet had not been out to see her sister in nearly three years. They'd met several times in other settings. Once at their parents' house in Maine, once in New York City with their sister Miranda and once Desi had come to L.A. for a conference and stayed with Juliet.

Desi's beloved wolves, housed in the sanctuary that was the most important thing in the world to her, had been there the last time Juliet visited, as had the cabin. The path still wound through a thick forest of ponderosa pines and across a grassy meadow where once Juliet had seen seven elk grazing on a summer morning. A string of mineral springs tumbled down the hill, their clear green waters steaming in the cold day.

"Hey, Juliet, did you see?" Desi said, pointing. "We built a grotto, just for you."

"Oh!" Juliet halted in delight. In small clearing, surrounded by red-trunked pines that gave off the scents of butterscotch and vanilla, was a pool steaming boldly in the cold afternoon. Boulders clustered at one end, and Juliet could see the care they'd taken to make the rest of the rocks appear as if Mother Nature had tossed them there for the convenience of the bathers. There was even a small waterfall at one end. "It's amazing, Desi!"

"You'll love getting in it even more, I promise," Desi said. "Very healing. It'll be good for both of us."

Juliet ducked her head. She knew Desi meant well, but she didn't see how sitting in *any* kind of water could possibly heal a mental wound unless it could erase a memory.

"I can't wait."

"Put a little enthusiasm in you voice, there, sis," Desi drawled.

Wryly, Juliet smiled. "I'm sure it will be wonderful."

As if he scented the newcomers, a wolf suddenly howled, a mournful sound cutting through the snowy afternoon. Next to Juliet, Glory stopped and lifted her chin to the sky, letting go of an eerily beautiful howl finished with a series of little yips.

Juliet smiled. "What did you say to him?"

Glory dipped her head coyly, danced, holding on to Juliet's hand, and yipped some more. In the distance, the wolves answered.

Desi paused and turned around. "They're talking back to you, Glory. Do you hear them?"

"I know! That's why I said it!"

"Said what?" Josh asked.

The little girl looked upset and embarrassed and Juliet wanted to protect her from whatever was intruding on the pretty little story she was telling herself. "If it's a secret," Juliet said, "you certainly do not have to tell us."

"I was telling them," Glory said quietly, "that we were bringing the princess to see them!"

"Glory likes to be a wolf," Josh said, coming up beside them. "Sometimes she only speaks in wolf for a whole day."

Juliet chuckled. "I bet that's interesting for you."

"Oh, yeah." He glanced down at her, his dark eyes twinkling. "Since I don't speak wolf at all."

"And I would imagine that translators are somewhat hard to come by." She grinned, feeling her guard slip just a little as she met his gentle gaze. For a moment, she didn't look away, only allowed the slight, easy connection, liking the size of him, his broad shoulders, his legs like tree trunks, a surety of movement as he placed one foot squarely, solidly, then the other.

When the small group entered the clearing where wolves lived, the creatures set up a wild greeting, rushing to the front of their roomy, sturdy kennels, wolves and wolf-mixes bred with a dozen kinds of dogs.

"Wow!" Juliet paused, amazed at how much work Desi had done here, too. There were a lot more kennels—really wide-open, fenced spaces, and a lot more wolves, and Juliet could see that Desi had sunk some serious money into the center. Her love for the animals showed. It almost seemed to Juliet that the wolves got preferential treatment. There were sheds and shelters, trees and water troughs in each kennel—and most important, a lot of room to roam and run. Toward the north, on the flat side of the mountain, was a low, rambling adobe building. It, too, was new. The lights were on.

A youth of about nineteen, with a Prince Valiant haircut and the long limbs of a grasshopper, carried a bucket down the dirt alleyway between kennels. "Glad to see you, boss," he said as he approached. "The new bitch is not eating at all."

Desi nodded. "I'll go check her out in a minute. Alex, I'd like you to meet my sister Juliet. Alex is a wolf-charmer."

"Oh, no," the young man said, his cheekbones going red. "She keeps saying that."

"She doesn't give compliments lightly," Juliet said, extending her hand. "You must be very good."

"Desi's been dying for you to get here." He leaned over as he shook her hand, his knobby wrist sticking out of his coat. "Nice to meet you."

"Thanks."

"Hey, Uncle," Alex said to Josh, then to Glory, "And to you, too, little sister."

Glory danced, high on her toes, and held tight to Juliet's hand. She howled in greeting.

Alex howled back. "Do you want to help me with the water?"

"Can the princess come with me?"

Alex gave Glory a quizzical look. "The princess?"

"That would be Princess Juliet," Josh said, putting his hand on her shoulder. Heavy. Warm. Enormous.

"Ah. The *princess.* Sure, she can come. I bet you want to see the wolves anyway, don't you?"

"Absolutely."

He led them down the dirt alley between fences. Wolves ran over curiously, in groups of two or three, occasionally more. Juliet remembered that wolves, in general, liked to be in a family group. Some were fine with a pair bond; others liked a pack.

"This is Persephone," Alex said, pausing beside a kennel where a wolf with thick, black and white-speckled fur huddled to the back. She raised her head when she heard voices, the gold eyes showing hope. When she saw who it was—evidently not who she had been hoping for—she sighed and put her head back down on her paws, despondence dripping from every hair. "She's not doing well here. We're trying to encourage her to bond with some of the other wolves, but it's not working."

Juliet moved closer, drawn to the sorrow of the animal. "Where did she come from?"

"She was abandoned by her owner, and was killing rodents and other small animals down in Gunnison before animal control picked her up. The woman at the humane society there recognized that she was a wolf, not a dog, and gave us a call."

"Is she as depressed as she seems?" Juliet asked.

He nodded. "A wolf bonds for life, you know? And when humans abandon them, they can take it pretty hard. She's the worst we've had for awhile."

"Poor thing," Josh said. He stood right behind Juliet, and his voice resonated through his chest in a velvety roll she felt on her shoulder blades. "What do you do?"

"Sometimes, you can introduce a pup or another wolf and they get better. Sometimes, they transfer the bond to another human, though this one has shown no interest in anyone yet. Sometimes," he shrugged, "they just die."

Juliet snapped her head up. "They die of a broken heart?"

Alex nodded and looked back at Persephone.

"Wow." Josh moved, and Juliet found herself exchanging a look with him. Up close, she noticed that he smelled almost the same as the forest floor, of loamy ground and pine needles and that essential otherness of mountain earth. As if he were somehow shaped of the land.

Quit it! She shouldn't be thinking the things she was thinking about him. She had a fiancé! Feeling unsettled, she looked back to the wolf. "How did you know her name was Persephone?"

"We named her that," Alex said. "For the goddess who was taken under the earth by Hades before she was returned."

"Beautiful."

The wolf lifted her head for a moment, listening. It almost looked as if she'd weep. Juliet turned away, a thick sensation in her throat. "I think I'm going to head back. I'm pretty tired."

"Princess, will you come see me?" Glory asked.

"Yes," she said. "Soon."

Chapter 3

As the two sisters settled in over a supper of beef stew and crusty bread, Desi asked, "So, how're you doing, Juliet?"

"Fine." Juliet thought of the soap operas and M&M's and the routine of meals and forced a bright smile. "Good! Really."

"How much longer until you go back to work?"

Juliet chased a carrot coin with her spoon. "I'm not sure."

"Which means?"

"It was—um—a forced leave of absence, Desi. Until I can get myself together, I don't need to show up."

Desi put down her spoon, her dark eyes peering right by all of Juliet's defenses. "I see," she said. For a minute, it seemed she might say something else, but she only gave a small nod, picked up her bread and tore off a piece. "Well, then, I guess it's a good thing that you came out here to visit me."

"I'm so glad to be here, Desi." Juliet impulsively touched her sister's hand. Her nails were short and functional, the knuckles a little raw from scrubbing them so often. "You didn't have to wait until it was completely crazy to call me, you know. You don't always have to be the strong one."

Desi looked stricken. "I'm only getting divorced, Juliet!"

"Only? Desi, your whole life is turned upside down!"

"Oh, it's not that." She scowled at her bowl. A lock of wavy dark hair feel against a cheek that was too white. "I mean, it's rotten, the divorce. But it's not the same as being the victim of a violent crime."

"It's been a year. I'm doing okay. And it's not a contest, anyway. You've been with Claude for what, fifteen, sixteen years?"

"I was twenty-one when I joined the Peace Corps and we met the day I arrived in Africa, so—" she flipped her fingers, counting mentally "—fifteen years, I guess."

"That's a long time. And he's really been terrible."

Desi nodded.

Juliet picked up her spoon. "Tomorrow, we'll go to town and start the paperwork—first the restraining order, then we'll find a divorce lawyer in town to help you out."

"Thanks. That's a good idea." She buttered a corn

muffin and flashed a sideways grin, an expression that made an elusive dimple appear. "And you can stop in and see Glory's red shoes, Ms. Princess."

Juliet thought of the little girl's wide-eyed adoration with a sense of warmth. "She made my day, that kid."

"She really does *not* like strangers. It's weird how much she likes you."

"Gee, thanks!" Juliet said with a laugh.

"You know what I mean. She's afraid of strangers. Her mother kidnapped her and she was missing for nearly eight months. Josh only got her back a few months ago."

"That sounds grim."

"I haven't heard all the details, but I gather it wasn't great. No abuse, but a lot of neglect and a lot of people in and out." Desi shook her head. "I don't understand a mother who would put her child in danger that way."

"No, I don't, either," Juliet said. "So he's not married?"

"Nope. And says he never will be again. He and I have formed a Better Friends Than Lovers club." She raised an eyebrow. "One luscious creature, isn't he?"

"It's not that." Juliet felt the tips of her ears get hot. "Well, I guess he is, you know, but I do have a fiancé."

"Nothing wrong with admiring the scenery."

"True."

"How is Scott, anyway?"

Juliet pasted on her bright social smile. "Fine."

Desi blinked. "You are *so* lying."

Juliet ducked her head. "You're right. Things are just not good. I'm not sure why—if it's me or it's him, or both of us." She opened her hands, palms up, and stared at the pinkish flesh around the perimeter. "Or what."

"You have been to a counselor, haven't you?" She frowned. "Rape isn't something you just get over in a day."

"I know. And yes, I've seen a counselor. " Juliet shook her head. "I'm really okay, Desi. It's been a year. It's not like I walk around thinking about it all the time. I've got some issues, but I'll get through them."

"But Scott has issues, too."

Juliet nodded. "I guess it's not uncommon for men to feel unsettled by the rape of a wife or girlfriend."

"Is he pushing you away?"

"Not at all. He—" She paused. "Hovers. It drives me crazy."

"Have you ever told Mom?"

"No. And I won't." Pushing her plate away, Juliet sighed. "Can we not discuss this anymore? Honestly, my girlfriends tiptoe around me and everyone at the law firm acted like I was a very delicate egg they might break. I'm *fine*."

Desi looked at her for a long moment, the dark eyes probing and still. "Well, it's a good thing," she said at last, "because I am a wreck and I need you."

"So do your wolves. I'm so proud of you for that sanctuary."

"That sanctuary is why I'm fighting Claude so hard for the land."

"How does he have any right to this land at all?" Juliet asked in outrage. "You bought it, didn't you?"

Desi shrugged. "I put the original down payment on it, but Claude has done a lot of work to it—clearing and building. He does have some claim, but Juliet—you have to help me with this part. If he takes the land, he'll just sell it to developers."

"Usually, there's a split. Is there some sort of equitable split you can work out?"

"Not easily." Desi bowed her head. "Not and protect the wolves."

"Can you buy him out?"

A glitter danced in Desi's eyes. "Well, I'm sure that's what he wants." The dimple in her cheek appeared. "Real estate prices have skyrocketed the past five years, and there isn't much buildable land available. With the hot spring and the meadows, this really is extremely desirable, and there's a developer who has offered almost ten million for it."

Juliet's mouth fell open. "Ten million?"

"I can't believe it, either—that's about 60 times as much as we paid for it ten years ago."

"How vulgar," Juliet said with a grin, imitating what their mother would say whenever people spoke of money. Still, she whistled. "That's a lot of money."

"It is. But I'm not selling. If I did, I'd betray everything I've been working for my whole life. The land shouldn't belong only to the rich."

"You're right." Juliet frowned. The value of the land complicated the divorce in a very sticky way. "But if you think the pressure will ease, you're crazy."

"I know." She rubbed her face. "It's insane."

"What happened to kick the real estate value so high so fast?"

"Couple of things. One is just that Colorado is such a great ski center, and one by one, all the major recreational areas are exploding. This ski area has been here for about twenty years, but it's hard to get here and with so many other choices, there was no rush to get to Mariposa."

"Which is why you guys liked it, right? It was the mountains, there's a town, but it wasn't a big mass of tourists."

"Exactly." She stood up and carried the bowls to the counter and put a stopper in the drain. "That, and even for Colorado, it's amazingly beautiful." Taking a teakettle off the stove where it had been warming while they ate, she poured hot water into the sink. "It's a lot of things that made the land skyrocket, but the big one is that Johann Larsen—the skier—started training here about seven years ago, and then he won all those medals at the Olympics. Now it's becoming a center for training."

"Yeah, but that would account for the value tripling, or even quadrupling. Not sixty-times-ing."

Desi raised her eyebrows. "They built a casino on the reservation."

"Ah." That would do it, combined with everything else. Juliet pursed her lips in thought. "That complicates things a lot. But we'll figure something out."

"I'm tired tonight, though, and I'm sure you are, too. Let's make some hot chocolate and curl up with the dogs inside and tell ghost stories."

Juliet rubbed her foot on Crazy Horse, a black lab mix who had the sweetest eyes in the world. "Can Crazy Horse sleep with me?"

Desi grinned. "Absolutely."

"Let's get some rest then." Juliet had a feeling they were going to need it, to deal with all the layers of this sticky divorce.

It was only as she was drifting off to sleep that she realized she'd forgotten to call Scott. And the slight pinprick of guilt only lasted a second, while the recognition of Desi's situation sank in.

Ten million dollars.

Good grief.

Josh would never understand the vagaries of the human female, whether she was four years old or four hundred. The morning was cold and sharp as cactus needles, but what did Glory come out of the room wearing? A short skirt and sandals with flowers.

And a crown.

"Glory," he said, putting forks on the table, "it snowed last night. Snow is cold. Go back and find something warm to put on."

"Like what? Grandma says you should help me pick stuff out."

"Grandma is a troublemaker." His mother, Helene, wanted Glory to be spit-polished every morning, with matching ribbons and socks. Josh had neither the time nor the talent to make that happen. "Don't you tell her I said that, either." The water on the stove was boiling. He poured a cup of old-fashioned oats into the pan. Patiently, he said, "Every time I help you, you complain."

"I want help this morning."

"Okay, go get a pair of jeans and a—" he had to stop

and think. Did everything go with jeans? "A blue sweater."

"I want a yellow sweater."

"Yellow, then, I don't care."

Glory marched back to her bedroom, muttering to Pink and Ink, her imaginary friends. She didn't allow anyone else to talk to them, and she was disgusted if an adult pretended to see them. At the same time, they were quite real in Glory's universe. As far as Josh could figure, Pink was a fluffy girl being, and Ink was a boy, sleek as a seal. Thcy wcre sister and brother.

"Spirit guides," his mother had pronounced in her I-am-the-Medicine-Woman voice.

"Named Pink and Ink?" Josh scoffed.

"Names don't matter."

He let it go. Helene was a sage and healer, in both "white" medicine and traditional native medicine. In the mainstream world, she was an emergency room nurse at the medical center, and on the reservation, she was a medicine woman, using a combination of spiritual and physical healing techniques like sweats and teas and spiritual journeys he no longer believed in.

But it worked for her. That was how he'd met Desi, actually, through his mother. They held women's sweats and drummings on Dcsi's land, in a sweat lodge by the hot springs. It was, evidently, sacred ground and Desi had been honored to help provide space.

"Hurry up, Glory!" Josh called. "Breakfast is almost ready."

Glory came out wearing a pink sweatshirt with a sequined butterfly over the front, and pale blue corduroy pants. Exasperated, he almost said something about the fact that she had not listened to his clothing advice, but let it go.

She handed him a brush. "Will you do my hair for me?"

"Definitely." He took the silver plastic-and-rhinestone tiara off her head and gave it to her to hold, then brushed out her long, thick hair. Sparks of static popped and flashed in the depths. When it was free, it fell past her hips in a perfectly straight waterfall of silk, but Glory liked it to be braided. He loved the cool weight of it weaving through his fingers. "You look very pretty," he said.

"I would like to get some curlers. Natasha has curls sometimes."

"Might have to take that up with Grandma. I'm not sure I know how to do curls."

She sighed, leaning against his knee as he braided her hair. "That's why a girl needs a mommy, too. Because dads don't know stuff."

She was only four. She didn't know it killed him to be so inept at the girly parts of parenthood. He did his best, but—again—he was a guy. He liked big messy things. Football games in muddy fields, big trucks with noisy engines, skinning fish. He didn't know much about making a living room look pretty or cooking anything beyond the basic meat and potatoes and oatmeal, though he was learning, painfully and slowly. He didn't know how to match clothes or do fancy braids.

He had, however, learned to paint her teeny-tiny fingernails. He'd even managed to get a miniscule star more or less centered on her thumbnail.

"Yeah, it's rough, kid," he said, fastening her braid. "You only have thirty-nine aunts and cousins and grandmas. One of them will know."

"The princess will know."

Josh felt a frisson of nervousness over his neck. Worry that Glory was flinging herself too much into this whole Juliet business, worry that someone else might let her down, worry that he couldn't protect her from everything no matter how much he might want to. "Well, if we see her, we'll ask her."

"We'll see her," Glory said. "She promised. Princesses keep their promises."

"I'm sure they do if they can, sweetie, but they have a lot of business to take care of, too."

Glory climbed up to the table. With a direct gaze that was much older than her years, she said, "We'll see her." She put the crown back in place on her head. "Stop worrying."

He chuckled and took the pot of oatmeal from the stove. "I'll do my best, kiddo. Do my best."

Juliet awakened to discover the warm breath of a dog on her neck. She didn't immediately realize it was a dog, only surfacing slowly to the warm weight of Tecumseh slumped against her body. She remembered his jumping up on the futon beside her during the night, and her welcoming his furry friendliness; she flung an arm around him and fell into the deepest sleep she'd known in months. No one could hurt you if they had to cross a seventy-five-pound wolf-mix to get to you.

But now that dog was panting against her neck. Politely at first, then with a cold nose against her ear, a quick nudge. When Juliet buried her head, Tecumseh put his paw on her shoulder.

"Okay, okay," Juliet said, and flung the covers back, wincing at the cold. The floor was freezing, the air as brisk as icicles. She spied Desi's down coat on a hook and put it on, and some boots that were resting by the stove, which had obviously either gone out or was very, very low. Juliet could see her breath. No wonder Desi had such long hair. She needed it for warmth!

Trying to move quietly, she shuffled toward the front door and let out the dog—well, dogs, now, since the other two were happy to have the chance to get outside, too. Desi locked the dog door at night. They moved gingerly, then one saw something in the trees and bolted. The other two followed in exuberant explosion, barking happily.

Juliet watched for a moment, then turned away to close the door and spied something out of the corner or her eye—a dark splash against the snow on the edge of the porch. She turned back frowning, and saw that it was a dead bird.

No, not just dead.

Murdered. Its throat had been cut.

Juliet yelped. Desi was at her side in two seconds flat, somehow alerted to danger by that small sound. She took one look at the dead bird and cursed. "Damn him!"

She stomped out on the porch, and picked the bird

up with a shovel. "I'm going to report this," she said, and settled the poor thing on top of the wood shed.

To Juliet's surprise, there was a tear in Desi's eye. "Are you okay?"

"No!" Desi said. "It's not okay to kill something to try to scare me, and I'm particularly fond of ravens, a fact that bastard knows, and used to hurt me."

Juliet hugged her. "Don't," she whispered. "Don't let him get inside of your head. He's being terrible, but one day this will all be over and your life will be good again."

Desi clutched her. "Promise?"

"I promise."

"Let's get ready to go to town." They dressed and did a few chores and piled into Desi's truck. "I'll treat you to breakfast before we get down to business," she promised. "Waffles and bacon?"

"Perfect."

Neither sister was particularly chipper first thing in the morning, and the dark spiritedness of the dead raven hung in the air. They rode in silence.

But after a few minutes, Juliet found herself admiring the scenery. It was so astonishingly beautiful it didn't seem real.

Thc storm had moved on, leaving behind enough snow to dust the trees and ground with a diamond sparkle. Sunshine beamed into the high mountain valley and the sharp, craggy peaks of the San Juans were newly touched with snow. "Do you ever get used to it?" she asked.

"The scenery? No way," Desi said. "How could you?"

"Good." She peered upward—up, up, up—to the

rugged red cliffs edged with stark white, and above them, the piercing blue of the sky. "I would hate to become immune. Every winter, I'd dream about being here. We never did come to ski, though, did we?"

"We begged enough, but I think our illustrious parents—" her voice was thick with irony "—thought it too plebian. If one were to ski in Colorado, it had to be Aspen, or at the very least, Vail."

"Is the camp still open?" All three sisters, Desi, Juliet and their youngest sister, Miranda, had come to camp in Mariposa every summer for years while their parents, afforded long vacations by their positions as college professors, stayed with friends in Crete, or hosted their set in Zurich, or ambled around whatever destination was approved for intellectuals that year.

"I think so. I see kids pouring into town on the bus every June."

"Poor things."

Desi laughed. "I loved coming to camp."

"I liked a lot of things about it, but I didn't like the bugs or the wild animals. I was scared all the time."

"You were?" Desi said in surprise. "I didn't know that. Why didn't you tell me?"

"Because you were always so brave about everything. Nothing scared you."

"I was always an outdoor kind of girl, though. You weren't."

"True." She admired the vividness of the sky. "What I really hated was being away from home all summer. It was really lonely."

"You poor baby!" Desi smiled. "You know me,

though—I loved getting away from…" She paused. "Oh, let's not be coy. I loved getting away from our parents. I couldn't wait. Camp seemed a thousand times more real and reliable than anything at home."

"I got used to it eventually." Juliet thought of those summers, her own wish to lean on reliable things, like the same room, the same stuff, the same friends, and Desi's adventurous heart, which had led to her travels abroad, and Claude. "What happened to Claude?" she mused aloud. "He always seemed like such a good guy."

Desi said carefully, "Do you think so?"

"Yeah. Don't you?"

"Yeah. I've just been wondering lately if I was blind or foolish or something." She gave Juliet a little shrug. "I'm glad you liked him, too."

Juliet reached over and touched Desi's shoulder. "You've always been wise and kind, Desi. Something changed Claude and his character didn't keep up."

"Thanks."

As they came down off the mountain and around a bend, they emerged suddenly from the trees and there was the narrow, long town of Mariposa. Five blocks wide, a mile and a half long. The sun had just climbed over the peaks to the east and now spilled into the valley, sparking on the snow-covered roofs. Juliet looked at her watch. Almost 8:30. "I bet it's dark on winter mornings."

"Very. The sun doesn't come up until nine." She swung onto the main street. Once it had been called simply Main Street, but it had been changed to Black Diamond Boulevard when the ski runs were built in the late seventies.

The tone of the town was half glitzy ski resort, half

mountain rustic. Stone bungalows built at the turn of the century populated the old part of town, along with buildings that dated back to gold rush days. At the ends of town, built to the very edge of the National Forest lands, were blocks of modern condos and faux Alpine shops housing restaurants and art galleries and shops selling sports gear and yoga clothing. Above it all rose the ski slopes.

"Uh-oh," Desi said. "There's Claude. Damn."

Juliet saw him ambling down the street in a black fleece vest and jeans and boots, his black braid shining. He held hands openly with a woman who wore what Juliet thought of as an adventure racer's uniform: tight stretchy pants with racing stripes down the side, a bright yellow thermal shirt, sunglasses on her tousled blond curls.

"Hey," Juliet said, recognition dawning, "isn't that Christie Lundgren? The skier?"

"Yep," Desi said, grimly. "Bastard! Now he has to make a fool of me in public?"

In alarm, Juliet looked up. "Just keep driving, Dez. You don't want any trouble."

But it was too late. Desi swung into a parking spot in front of the bank, and threw open the door before Juliet could so much as blink. Desi had something in her hands. Juliet couldn't make out what it was at first, but then she saw it was a phone. A camera phone. Desi dashed in front of the couple and snapped a picture, then another, before Claude managed to disentangle himself from his girlfriend.

Juliet got out of the truck, braced for anything.

But Desi grinned in triumph, waving the camera over her head. "Got you now, you sorry rat."

"What difference will a picture make?" Claude said.

"Date and time stamped? Plenty." She saluted the blond skier next to Claude. "Enjoy," she said, and headed back to the truck. Juliet, shivering in her thin coat, gladly headed back toward the truck. Out of the corner of her eye, she saw Claude make a sudden move. Juliet whirled.

Claude dived for Desi, who yelped, leaping a little to try to get away from him. He managed to grab the sleeve of her coat, and they slid around on the snow underfoot. Desi cried, "Juliet! Come get this!"

Juliet, shaken out of her surprise, dashed toward her sister. "Throw it!"

But Claude grabbed Desi close to him, and the two of them wrestled, slipping and sliding on the snow, and Desi couldn't get her arm free. "Let me go!" Desi cried.

"You owe me," Claude roared. "You're not going to cheat me out of that land. I bought it, too."

A crowd started to gather, across the street in front of the diner, and in the street. "I bought that land with my inheritance from my grandmother, and you know it." She yanked free suddenly, and started to bolt. "Juliet!" she cried, but Claude tackled her.

The two of them went down, slamming hard into the pavement. The girl with him yelped and plastered her back against the wall. Juliet saw blood spill brightly into the snow, but couldn't see who it belonged to. She rushed toward them. "Stop it, you two!" Juliet yelled. "Just stop it!"

Claude cried out and jumped up, the phone in his hand. Blood streamed out of cuts on his lip and cheekbone, and he wiped it away angrily. With a guttural cry of victory, he dropped the cell phone on the stone stoop and smashed it beneath the heel of his boot.

Desi, too, was bleeding from a cut in her scalp, and tears poured down her face. She struggled to her feet as Claude walked away. "I'm going to *kill* you, Claude Tsosie," she cried after him.

"You can try," he said, turning around to smirk at her.

Furiously, Desi bent down, picked up a rock, and threw it after him. It landed harmlessly a few feet behind him, but Desi slipped and landed on her bottom. Stunned, she didn't move, an expression of bewilderment and grief on her face.

Blood from the cut on her head stained the shoulder of her coat, and Juliet bent down with tenderness. "Come on, honey," she said gently, helping her sister to her feet. "Let's get you to the doctor."

A tall Ute woman with craggy dark features materialized on the street, a clean white towel in her hands. She pressed the cloth to the wound. "Desi, Desi," she said in a voice that sounded like the soft south wind, "you must let him go."

"I need to take care of the wolves," Desi said, wearily. "If he takes half the land, I can't."

"The law will be on your side," the woman said. She met Juliet's eyes. "Let's get her to the clinic. She's gonna need stitches."

Juliet nodded. "And then, we are going to file properly for divorce, and for a restraining order to keep you two apart until this is over, got it?"

Desi bowed her head. "Yes."

Chapter 4

The scalp wound needed six stitches, but as it was Mariposa, a clinic that was supremely qualified to treat cracked heads, and it was the between season—between the high hiking and high skiing periods—it only took a half hour from start to finish. Then Desi, her friend Helene, the Ute woman, and Juliet were finally having breakfast at the Red Buffalo, a diner on Black Diamond Boulevard.

It was a busy morning. Several times, people stopped by the table to ask about Desi's bandaged head, and the trouble that had caused it. Others gave a quick nod and hurried by, and Juliet realized the town's people were taking sides. Some on Desi's side, some on Claude's.

Damn.

Desi noticed, too. "He's so damned charming and

good-looking," she said, matter-of-factly. "It's hard to get people to see beyond that."

"It's why some politicians can get so far," Juliet said.

"What's the feeling about Claude on the rez, Helene?" Desi asked. "They like him there?"

Helene lifted a shoulder. "Some do, the same ones who like him around town here. The ones who fall for charm and good looks fall for him, even in Indian Country." She stirred her coffee. Her wrist, flat and strong and brown, was ringed with three beaded bracelets in different colors. "There's some who like him 'cause he's been successful. Others don't because of the same thing."

"Why would they not like him because he's successful?" Juliet asked.

"Some people want everybody to suffer together."

Juliet frowned. "I'm still not quite getting why all this fuss about the two of you, anyway? Why does anyone care?"

"Because the land is so valuable," Helene said.

"But why would anyone on the reservation care about that?"

"In a town this small," Desi said, "everyone is intimately connected. Our fortunes are all mixed up together. The politicians will care what the Indian community wants because the casino is such a cash cow, and the Indian vote is huge."

"The lawyers will care because they want to be politicians," Helene said. "The townsfolk care because they need things to keep their tongues wagging, and everything financial ripples around the whole town."

Desi smoothed the empty spot on her left hand where her wedding ring had lived. "The businessmen will care because they court the Indian vote so the politicians will swing their way on land decisions."

"Are there businessmen trying to get the land right now?"

Desi snorted. "Oh, yeah. Developers of all kinds."

Juliet's head ached the slightest bit. "This is a lot more complicated than I expected." She rubbed the spot between her brows, thinking of what needed to be done.

First, she needed to do some research, both on local real estate law and practices, and on cases like this one in recent courts. "Have you talked to a lawyer at all, Desi?"

"Who can I trust around here, really? The lawyers all want to be politicians, the—"

"I get it."

A happy little cry cut through the gloom at their table. "Hi, Grandma!" said a girl who popped up at the edge of the booth.

"Glory, what are you doing here? Why aren't you at preschool?" Helene asked, clearly surprised to see her granddaughter. No more surprised than Juliet was to realize Helene was Glory's grandmother.

"My teacher had a toothache."

"Oh, that's too bad." Helene scooted over to let the little girl, with her long dark braid, into the booth beside her.

As Glory scrambled in, adjusting a tiara tucked with bobby pins into her hair, she happened to glance up and see Juliet. "Princess!" she screeched. "What are you doing here?" Before Juliet could answer, she whipped her head up to her grandmother. "How do *you* know the princess?"

"This is weird," Desi said.

Juliet liked it. She liked it even more when rumble-voiced Josh strolled up to the table and gave her a nod. "How are you, Princess?"

She smiled. His eyes were as warm and kindly as she remembered from yesterday. "Not bad. How are you?"

"Glad to see you. This little girl—" He took a breath. "*Believes,* you know?"

Juliet nodded. "It's okay."

He caught sight of Desi's bandaged head. "What happened to you?"

"Long story." Desi stood up, vacating the spot next to Juliet. "Sit down, Josh. I'm going to go wash my hands."

"I've got to get to the dojo in a few minutes—a home-school class is coming." But he sat down anyway, the long, solid weight of him warm against Juliet's side. His hands were as big as saucers, and he folded them together in front of him. He wore no jewelry on them. Juliet thought they were extraordinarily beautiful, the sinews and lines, the graceful length of his fingers, the oval nails.

In her fluting voice, Glory said, "Princess, do you want to come sit by me?"

Juliet looked away from Josh's hands. "Honey, we have to run some errands in a few minutes."

Her radiant face dimmed. "Oh."

Juliet leaned forward. "I'll be finished in an hour or two. I can come see you later, if you like. You can show me your red shoes."

"Hey! That's a good idea! Grandma, can you take me

to my house in a couple of hours so I can show the princess my shoes?"

Helene grinned, her eyes crinkling into angles. "I can do that."

"Okay."

"What happened to Desi's head?" Josh asked.

"She…uh…fell down."

He flipped a butter knife end to end on the table. "Claude somehow mixed up in it?"

"Yeah." Juliet glanced at Helene. "Your mom was there, too. You can hear more about it later."

"I'm not deaf, you know," Glory said. "I know about grown-up fights, too. My mommy had them all the time."

"Nobody is keeping secrets, Glory," Josh said. "But even if we were, you are a little girl, and little girls don't need to know everything. We like to keep things nice for you."

Glory sighed, long-suffering, and with a harrumph, leaned her cheek into her hand.

Juliet chuckled. "I like your tiara," she said. "And I can't wait to see your shoes later."

"Me, too." She suddenly perked up. "Hey! Princess, do you know how to curl hair?"

"Sure. You want your hair curled?"

"Yes," Glory said emphatically. "Natasha in my class always has her hair curled and my daddy doesn't know how."

Josh put one hand beneath the table and squeezed Juliet's hand lightly. "Thanks," he said very quietly.

"No problem." She pulled free delicately, and Desi came back to the table.

"Ready?" her sister asked, putting sunglasses on her head.

"I am."

A woman in a yellow jacket moved by the table and gave Desi a long, hard glare. Desi stared right back. When the woman continued toward the cash register, Desi and rolled her eyes at Juliet. "The dentist's wife," she said when the woman had gone outside. "She hates my guts."

"Because?"

"Because she's one of Claude's groupies, and in their eyes, I'm just a mean woman who doesn't understand him."

"Yeah," Josh said, behind them, "you old meanie, you."

Desi grinned, her eyes flashing in a way that made her sister wonder what had forged the bond between these two.

And was there something romantic brewing? "You better believe it, mister."

Did her sister have feelings for this man? He was sort of her type, after all, a rugged Native American, an outdoorsman. He had that adorable daughter who needed a mother.

Josh laughed softly, and Juliet felt the sound run down her neck like warm fingers. She resisted looking up at him, getting caught again in that dark, patient gaze. But even as she resisted, she felt the steady presence of him at her back, solid, steady, calm, and she couldn't help the wave of yearning it kindled in her. It had been a long time since Juliet had felt safe—if she ever had.

Scott was a good man—smart, supportive, ambitious—but she'd never felt sheltered by him. Josh, on the other hand—

With a popping little shock, she heard her thoughts. *Stop it!* She was engaged! It was one thing to admire the long, sturdy thighs of a man, or the grace of his hands. A woman had eyes, after all....

But it was something else again to be thinking of resting against that broad shoulder, to imagine taking a deep breath of relief as that deep laughter rang into the room.

Disloyal. In two directions if Desi was attracted to him, too.

Blindly, Juliet stood and walked towards the door, grabbing a green-and-brown-wrapped mint from a bowl on the counter. "I'll be right outside," she called back. Without waiting for a reply, she rushed out.

The door was in a little foyer with racks of newspapers and tourist brochures on one side. As Juliet rushed through, a man was coming in, and Juliet stepped aside, and—

Slammed squarely into her demons. She was never quite sure what happened, why she was flung back in time, but suddenly, she smelled a musky aftershave and margaritas, and there was a swooshing of all sound, as if her ears were covered. In real time, she ducked her head and managed to stumble around the man coming in the door, ignoring him when he said, "Miss, are you all right?" and got out to the sunshine in the street. Sweat poured down the back of her neck.

But even in the bright sunshine and open air, her throat felt constricted, and her breath came in ragged, tearing gasps. The worst was the sense of mindless panic urging her to *flee! flee! flee!* Her legs burned with the need, her lungs felt as if they would explode. With as much control as she could muster, she grabbed the stone corner of the building and leaned on it, trying not to fight the sensations nor give into them.

A heavy hand fell on her shoulder. "Hey, Juliet, are you—"

She screamed, slammed the hand away. Tried to back off, bumped into the wall.

Saw that it was Josh, and wanted to burst into tears.

He held his hands up, palm out to show he wouldn't hurt her. "Hey, hey, hey," he said. That rich gentle voice splashed into her panic, coating it like chocolate.

And just as suddenly as she'd been sucked into the flashback, she fell back out. With a soft noise, Juliet pitched forward, instinctively reaching for the sturdiness of his big, strong shoulders. Her head landed against his sternum, and she could smell the clean freshness of clothes hung out to dry on a line, and something deeper, his flesh. A gentle light hand smoothed her hair.

"You're okay," he said. "You're okay."

And it was true. After a moment, the dark memories retreated, and she could take a long, slow breath. Raise her head. Only then did she realize how close they were. Embarrassed, she tried to take a step back, and bumped into the wall at her back. "I'm sorry," she said, trying to duck to her left, afraid to look at him.

"Easy." He moved his big hand up and down her arm. "You don't have to go anywhere. Your sister will be here in a hot second."

"I'm—this is…oh, I'm embarrassed." She bent her head. "Thanks. I'm sorry."

"You don't have to apologize." His rumbling voice again rolled down her spine, easing the tension there, and his hands kept moving on her arms in a most soothing way. Steady. Gentle. "You don't have to say anything at all."

Juliet bent her head. He wore dark brown leather hiking boots, sturdy-looking with laces and hooks and eyes and a sole that looked as if it could withstand six inches of ice. Her feet in their thin California boots looked insubstantial, tiny even, and with a glimmer of pleasure, she thought one of the reasons to like a man so big was so that you could feel small next to him. And she was not normally a small woman.

She wanted to offer an explanation, to say something to excuse her weird behavior. The flashbacks were hateful, like a scar, and it made her feel overwhelmed to imagine telling him. Where to start? "Thanks," was all she said.

He released her and in the next instant, Desi came out, offering breath mints to everyone. Juliet moved away, vaguely aware of him watching her. "We'd better get to the courthouse," she said. "Get this taken care of."

"Yep. Let's do it. "

Juliet glanced up at Josh. "See you later."

His eyes were steady and sober and saw far more than she wished. "Right."

The homeschoolers left after their weekly practice, and Josh took advantage of the fact that he had a day off from his job as a tribal policeman on the reservation—they worked three on and two off—and the fact that his mother had Glory for the morning to do some cleaning at the dojo. He could have hired a service to do the work for him, but he found the rote actions of dusting, sweeping, mopping to be a healthy way to order his own mind.

He opened the doors and windows to the blaze of fresh mountain air, sweetened by the now-melting snow. In predictable autumn capriciousness, the sun was now warm enough to warrant the dread-locked boys taking off their shirts.

There were several layers of things on Josh's mind this afternoon. The first was Desi and Claude. It was a dangerous situation and getting more dangerous by the hour. Until now, Claude had kept his little assignations quiet, or at least somewhat under the table, and although some of the ex-mistresses were a little volatile, Claude had managed to keep them under control. The new one, Christie Lundgren, was a well-known professional skier, a woman much younger than Claude, and well known for her scathing and destructive temper. By all accounts, she was wildly smitten with her handsome, artistic, exotic lover.

Now Claude had gone public, humiliating Desi and, Josh was afraid, others. Claude's layers of women were like those Russian dolls, another and another and another. Someone had been cast aside for Lundgren.

On the plus side, Lundgren had plenty of money from endorsements, and Claude would no doubt want to keep her happy. Maybe he'd accept the restraining order with something resembling respect, at least until the divorce settlement could be hammered out.

Or not.

Trading a feather duster for a spray bottle filled with vinegar and water and a bag full of clean rags, Josh sprayed the first of the big windows in the room. It had once been a mother-in-law house behind a bungalow. Josh had knocked out most of the internal walls to open it up, and hung mirrors along the far wall. These old windows had ancient glass, with ripples and imperfections he genuinely loved, and he liked the action of making them shiny.

The next thing on his mind was his daughter's absolute refusal to speak of her time with her mother at all. Not with a counselor, not with her grandmother, not with him. But sometimes in nursery school, she drew chaotic pictures that frightened her teacher, and sometimes, she still awakened screaming.

It killed him. If it was not against his practice, he would hate his ex-wife. He didn't know, had no way to know, what had transpired in the long months Glory had been missing. She was found in Denver, finally, when the house they were living in caught fire, and they were transported, along with the other eight people living in the house, to the hospital. A nurse recognized Glory from a flyer in the newspaper, and called the police, who took the little girl into custody. Glory had been too thin, easily startled, but there had been no evidence of any sort of abuse. She'd been almost heartbreakingly happy to see her father and rarely spoke of her mother ever after.

Sunlight, captured by a bubble in the old glass, blazed in the window he washed. Josh rubbed a circle around it, thinking. The way Juliet looked after breakfast made him think of Glory's blankness when her mother was mentioned.

Which brought him to the last thing on his mental agenda—his discovery that Juliet was wounded. Obviously. Painfully.

Which, in a word, sucked. He'd done his time with broken birds. He drew them in flocks for reasons he could never quite figure out, and inevitably, he tried to mend their cracked wings and broken hearts. Inevitably, he failed, the most dramatically with his ex-wife.

These days, there was only room in his life for one wounded bird, and that was his own daughter.

The trouble was, Glory had made up her mind that Juliet was the finest thing to fall to earth in eons. Josh couldn't bear to deny her the pleasure of Juliet's company. Perhaps it would be a healing thing for both of them. Maybe the wounded birds would heal each other.

In the meantime, he'd just have to keep himself a bit aloof, apart. Much as he'd like to, he couldn't afford to explore the depths of the lovely Juliet.

Chapter 5

Josh's resolve to stay aloof was immediately tested when Juliet showed up at the dojo an hour later. She'd obviously been shopping with Desi, because the pair of them came in wearing matching blouses, Desi in pink, Juliet in blue. He half grinned when they came in, laughing like girls. "Sorry, did we have a flashback to the hippie days?"

Desi laughed. Their blouses were airy Indian cotton embroidered with sequins and beads. "Everything in the stores is like this! It's like sixth grade all over again!" She spun around to model it, her long, long dark hair spilling down back, her curvy figure giving new meaning to the word *body.* "What do you think?"

"I think you ought to put on girl clothes more often."

He knew Desi rarely—if ever—indulged on clothes that could only be worn for fashion's sake, opting instead for more practical garb.

"That's what I told her," Juliet said.

Until she spoke, he'd managed to keep her blurred at the edges of his vision, a smear of blue and yellow in the corner of his eye. When she spoke, he had to look.

And then he couldn't look away. Everything about her looked floaty. Otherworldly, like a scarf that might blow away in a good wind. Her fine blond hair hung loose around her neck; the thin fabric of the blouse skimmed her slim shoulders and arms in a way that made him think of cobwebs.

She was…ethereal. Well, ethereal except the vivid turquoise of her eyes. And the lush, red bow of her mouth and the supple thrust of her breasts beneath the all-too-thin fabric. How could someone be so wispy and so lush at once?

"You look nice, too," he said. Did they notice the gruffness of his voice? He resisted clearing his throat. *Don't be an idiot, man. Ain't you ever seen a girl before?*

"Thanks." She held up the shopping bag she was carrying. "I hope you don't mind, but I brought Glory a present."

"You did?" He tried to hide his dismay, but evidently was not particularly successful. Juliet's cheeks turned red and Desi jumped in.

"It's my fault," she said. "We bought matching shirts for us, and for our sister in New York, and we decided to see if there was one in Glory's size."

"But it's okay, we can take it back, no problem," Juliet said. "It was presumptuous, I'm sorry."

"Naw, it's all right." He leaned on his broom, let a smile surface. "I'm just worried that she's gonna get her little heart broken, you know?"

Juliet put her hands to her chest. "Oh, I'd never break her heart! I promise."

She would never *mean to,* he could see that. He folded the rag in his hands, then refolded it, testing the sensation in his chest. Warning. But for was it for Glory, or for him? "She'll be tickled pink that you brought her a present, Princess."

"I've got to get some work done," Desi said, "check on a bull that was injured and touch bases with the clinic. You can stay here and visit with Glory, if you want. Give me a call on the cell—" She halted, frowned thunderously. "How am I going to function without a cell phone?"

Juliet raised her eyebrows.

"I'll have to go get a replacement." She growled. "That infuriates me!"

"Let it go," Juliet said.

Desi's hands flew in the air. "I know, I know." She pursed her lips. "Okay, when I get my new cell, I'll call you on yours, and then I can run by and pick you up later."

"Can I walk over to the clinic?" In addition to the wolf center, Desi had a traditional large animal practice in town. "I'd like to see it."

"Sure, it's at the east end of town, on the main road."

She gave walking directions. "Still, let me know you're coming, okay? So you're not stuck waiting for me forever and I don't even know. I'll finish up and then we'll head back to the house."

"Trust me," Josh said, "you want to call her."

"Okay. I've got the number programmed into my cell." Juliet pulled it out of her purse to show them. "You guys are acting like I'm twelve. I live in Hollywood, remember?"

Desi laughed, and Josh thought it was the easiest-sounding sound that had come from her in months. It was good for her to have Juliet around. "Did you get everything taken care of this morning?" he asked.

"Yes. Restraining order filed. Divorce papers picked up and will be filed by the end of the week, so we can get that rolling." She held up three fingers. "Scout's honor."

"Good work."

"Thanks." Desi put on her coat and headed for the door, rattling her keys as she waved. "See you kids later."

When she left, the bell over the door ringing faintly, Juliet looked at Josh and said, "I'm sorry about the little scene at the restaurant. That hasn't happened for awhile."

"You don't have to apologize," he said again. "It's okay."

She started to speak, then stopped, putting her hands in her back pockets. A pose that neatly illuminated the curve of her waist. For a long moment, she searched his face with narrowed eyes, and he had a chance to simply meet that blue gaze. He took in the tiny scar through her left eyebrow, and what looked like a chicken pox scar on her chin, barely visible and strangely appealing.

At last she nodded. "That's a relief. Thanks."

"No problem. Let's go find Glory, Princess Juliet."

Juliet stepped out into the day and blinked, wishing for her sunglasses. With one hand, she shielded her eyes and lifted her head to the brilliant blue sky. "Wow."

Josh raised his gaze, chuckled. "That about says it, all right."

Down the mountains spilled gleaming waterfalls of yellow aspens, vivid against the darker pines. It looked as if a pot of paint had tipped over. "I keep trying to name that color in my head—yellow doesn't really capture it, and lemon is too bright and it's not quite like butter."

"Marigold?"

"Closer," she agreed. "Saffron, maybe?"

"I'm not sure I know what saffron is."

"A spice. It's a little muddy, though. Marigold or sunflower are much closer." She dropped her hand, gave him a quick smile. "Sorry. I keep stopping to rhapsodize."

"Don't apologize. It's too easy to forget how amazing it is when you live here. We need the reminder to look around once in awhile." He gestured. "I never drive in town, so we'll just walk over to my mother's. It's not very far."

"I'm glad to walk. It's an amazing day." She felt buoyed, effervescent, and wasn't sure if it was the weather or the altitude or maybe the company of the very handsome man beside her. "The weather changed so fast!"

"And it'll change again this afternoon," he said,

pointing toward the south. "Those clouds might bring some more snow with them."

A pair of dogs, one black, one salt-and-pepper, loped by on some happy errand, bandanas tied around their throats. One stopped to bark at a third dog leaning his head out of the window of a pickup truck, a dog with an enormous head, who simply looked down at the Lab and yawned.

"I've never seen so many dogs in a town in my life," Juliet commented.

"They issue you one when you come to town."

Juliet laughed.

His eyes glittered. "Haven't you gotten yours yet?"

"Please, Desi has three *big* dogs. That's plenty."

"All right, we'll let you slide for a bit."

They walked in agreeable silence up a short hill. "So, what sort of martial arts do you teach?" she asked.

"Kung fu, mostly."

"I like the eastern arts," she said, and hoped it didn't sound too prim. "I studied yoga and tai chi for awhile."

"Yoga makes me feel impatient," he said, and gave her a rueful smile. "I think I need to move more than that."

They stopped at Black Diamond Boulevard and waited for the traffic to thin. "It's really busy for a small town," Juliet said.

"Wait until winter comes. You'll have to fight to cross this street, even with stop signs at every corner."

Juliet started to say, *I won't be staying that long,* but how did she know? She wouldn't leave Desi until everything was stable. "I'll keep that in mind."

The light changed and they crossed the street, and

into a small pocket of cottages and bungalows tucked between the main drag and the northern mountain. "Why aren't there ski slopes on both sides of the valley?" Juliet asked.

He flipped a thumb over his shoulder to the south. "That one faces north, so the snow gets deeper and stays longer and doesn't get as icy." He pointed to the one in front of them. "The sun melts the snowfall on this one much faster."

She grinned. "Cool. I love it when I learn something new like that."

"So, you got things taken care of this morning with Desi?"

"I think so. You're very worried about it, aren't you?"

He made a clicking sound with his tongue. "Well, I'll tell you. I've been a cop a long time, and that relationship has all the danger signs."

Juliet felt a prickling of dread, a sense of warning. "What do you mean?"

"They're very intense people, both of them. And at one time, I gather it was very passionate."

"Yeah, that's the weird part. I would have said they loved each other a lot."

"It struck me as something a little different." He turned his lips down in thought, and Juliet found herself admiring the angle of his cheekbone, the grace of his throat. She looked toward the cerulean sky instead.

"Possessive," he continued. "They *possessed* each other. Claude bagged an upper-class white woman with a social conscience, a pretty woman with a lot of heart who'd make him look good wherever he went."

"And Desi?"

He hesitated, then quirked an eyebrow. "She got herself somebody good-looking enough for her tastes, and exotic enough to give her cachet, and made sure he was an artist to piss off your parents."

Juliet laughed. "Very acute observation, Mr. Mad Calf."

"It's a kind of love, meeting needs like that. Relationships are complicated things."

"My parents taught us that very young."

"They sound like pretty complicated people."

"Mmm. Complicated is one word for it." She shook her head. "Or dysfunctional."

He looked down at her. "Why do you say that?"

"They're just...very intense. It's a very intense relationship. They fight and make up and swear the other one is killing them and then they go off on some big trip and they're crazy about each other again." She shook her head. "It would be exhausting to live like that."

"And it wouldn't leave a lot of energy for the children," he commented.

"Bingo."

"Still, love is a complicated thing, as you said. Why do we fall in love? It would be nice if it was always with someone who would be good for you, who'd take care of you, bring out the best, all that—but how often does it really happen?"

"Are you speaking from experience?"

His smile was wry. "Definitely."

She frowned, thinking of Scott. Whom she had not

been thinking of enough. Was that a relationship based on love or need?

Until recently, she'd believed she loved him, but maybe it *was* more been a matter of convenience and suitability. He was a lawyer, she was a lawyer. They both liked having someone to go out to dinner with and to accompany each to various business functions. They'd traveled to appealing spots together on vacation—the lesser known islands of Hawaii, the less-Americanized east coast of Mexico, Belize. They understood the demands of the work schedule of a busy professional and neither was particularly upset when the other had to work.

Tidy, convenient, pleasant.

Or was that fair? He'd stuck by her after the rape. But it was still just a very polite relationship in ways.

The very opposite of her parents' relationship. But was that what she really wanted? Maybe it was possible to have something somewhere in between.

A thick tension rose in her chest. She felt guilty, not loving him after all he'd done. She wished she knew why she *didn't*.

"Here we are," Josh said, gesturing toward a stone house nestled close to the mountain rising behind it. It was made of reddish stone, with a small turret on the ground floor and a small second story. A deep wooden porch was furnished with chairs and a table, and a pot of winter-brushed marigolds stood in the middle of the table. Homey. A dog barked from a front window, only visible in silhouette.

"I see you have your dog, too."

"Jack," he agreed. "Told you, it's regulations."

The door burst open and Glory rushed out, her long licorice hair scattering free over her arms and back. "Hi, Princess! Come in. We made tea, me and my grandma." She flipped her hair. "Hi, Daddy. You can have some, too. If you want."

"Gee, thanks."

The dog came leaping out, too, a mutt of indeterminate parentage with long red fur and a big black head, and a lolling, happy tongue. He nosed her hand and wiggled around in a circle around Josh. "This," Josh said, "is Jack."

"Too many J's," Juliet said.

He laughed.

Glory took Juliet's hand. "Come inside, Princess," she said, gazing upward with naked admiration, and brushed hair out of her face. The little girl's small fingers were cool and dry, but very sure. "Come sit down."

The house smelled of lemons and cinnamon, and beneath that, something Juliet couldn't quite name, a little sweet and exotic. They entered a large living room furnished simply with a slightly threadbare couch, two chairs and a giant ottoman, all gathered around a potbellied stove. A round table sat beneath a very old drop light made of frosted glass, and a large window topped with leaded glass looked down the street to a perfectly framed view of the town and a tumble of aspens above it.

She turned around. "Butterscotch," she said to Josh.

He didn't understand immediately, then looked

over her shoulder to the view of aspens, and grinned. "You're right."

The expression transformed his face. His eyes crinkled up at the corners and a fan of sun lines radiated outward into his high-planed cheeks. Big strong teeth showed in a wide smile. Juliet felt an electric little zing through her chest.

Whoa. Careful there, she thought. Flustered, she bent and petted the dog, who had followed them into the room. He lay down at her feet, sighing hard. Juliet chuckled when he covered one of her arches. "Silly thing."

"Hello again," Helene said. "You must be very special—nothing would do but the most special of our cookies." She gestured with amusement to the plate of sugar cookies dusted with cinnamon and slices of yellow cake. "I hope you're hungry."

"Definitely."

Josh put his hand on her shoulder. "I have a few errands to run, so I'll leave you to the care of the females in my world, if you don't mind."

"We'll be fine," Helene said. "Run along."

A wave of disappointment washed over Juliet, and she had to paste a smile on her face. "We'll be fine."

As she helped herself to the tea and cookies, she told herself it was better this way. The less she saw of him, the wiser it would be. Even if she didn't have a fiancé—which she did!—she had other issues. So did Josh.

To the little girl awaiting her opinion of the feast, she

said, “Glory, I have never tasted such a delicious cookie in my life.”

Glory said in the way only a four-year-old could, “I know.” She leaned her hand on her chin. “Will you marry my daddy, Princess? Then I could have a mommy who was a princess.”

Helene said, “Glory, we don’t ask such personal questions.”

“It isn’t personal.”

Juliet said quickly, “Would you like to show me your red shoes before we forget?”

“Hey! That’s a good idea!”

Over Glory’s head, Helene mouthed, “Sorry!”

Juliet just shook her head and let a starstruck little girl lead her to the red shoes, feeling like a movie star or a…well, a princess.

After showing off her shoes and other treasures, including butterfly hair clips and a poster of Snow White, then having cookies and tea, Glory was glazed with overstimulation. Juliet tried to take her leave, thinking to make up an excuse so the poor thing could get a nap.

“Oh, don’t go yet, Princess,” Glory cried. “Auntie Desi’s not here. How’re you gonna get home?”

“What if you get me some books and we sit here and read?”

“Okay! Will you read to me? I have a whole book about princesses.”

Helene chuckled.

“Of course,” Juliet said.

Glory ran into the other room to find the book she

wanted, and Juliet helped Helene carry the dishes from the dining room into the kitchen. "She's a terrific little girl," Juliet said.

"Thanks. You must have experience with children. You're very good with her."

"I don't have any of my own, but I do some work at a center that offers services to displaced immigrant women. A lot of kids there."

Helene stacked plates into the dishwasher. "That sounds like interesting work. Do you like it?"

Scraping frosting and the shell of pistachio nuts into the trash, Juliet nodded. "Better than my actual job. That's a side job, pro bono work, but it feels like I'm really doing something when I'm there."

"Sometimes it happens that way—the side trip leads to the main road."

Startled, Juliet looked up. "I never thought of that."

Helene smiled and finished loading the dishwasher. She dried her hands on a cup towel. "Will you mind if I leave you with Glory now? Josh is supposed to be back within a half hour."

"That's fine."

Glory ran back into the kitchen, a picture book with a glossy cover under her arm. "I got my book."

"Okay, sweetie. Let's go read."

Chapter 6

The room was warm, the fire crackling at her feet. Juliet grew sleepier and sleepier, and she could tell when Glory slumped against her in a heavy slumber. Juliet put the book aside. She thought about the slight shock she got from reading about princesses falling in love with a prince at first kiss, the whole myth and shocking suddenness of it. No wonder, she thought drowsily, there was so much discontent in the world of romance. They'd all been fed this nonsense of love at first sight for the whole of their youth.

Cynic, said a little voice in her head. But Juliet could find no words to protest. Glory's head nestled against her shoulder. The dog snored lightly. The chair was deep and soft, her feet cradled on an oversize ottoman.

When she startled awake some time later, she had no

idea how much time had passed, but it was the sudden cold spot where Glory's warm body had been that alerted her. She sat straight up, blinking, to see Josh carrying the very asleep weight of girl in his arms.

"Hey, sleeping beauty," he said, his voice very soft.

She waved vaguely, surprised at how deeply she'd fallen asleep.

"Be right back," he mouthed.

Juliet rubbed sensation back into her right arm, and yawned. She must have fallen *really* asleep. The room was gloomy with late afternoon, and the fire had gone very low. Desi would be worried about her!

Jumping up, she tried to remember where she'd put her purse, and finally found it by the table. She dug in the pocket where she kept her cell phone and pulled it out. It was off; with a stab of guilt she turned it back on. The screen told her there were five missed calls.

Five? Yikes! How had she missed five calls?

Then it came to her. She'd turned the phone off yesterday on the plane and never turned it back on. Guiltily, she pushed the button to review the numbers before she picked up voice mail. The first was Scott, yesterday at 4:00 p.m., about the time Desi had been pointing a rifle at Claude. The second was Scott, about 9:00 p.m. last night. The third, Scott, this morning. Desi, number four. Scott number five, just a few hours ago.

She was about to punch the number for voice mail when Josh came back into the room. "Don't bother. I saw Desi about ten minutes ago, and she said to tell you she left a message on the phone to tell you she's going to be awhile. A farmer with some sick pigs."

"Oh." She closed the phone, feeling suddenly the enclosed silence of the room, the pair of them essentially alone.

He seemed to notice it, too. "Where'd my mom get off to?"

"She had to meet someone. She said to tell you to call her later."

"All right."

Silence dropped between them. Juliet rubbed her hands together. "Um. I hate to be a pain, but I don't really have anywhere to go until Desi comes to get me."

"You don't have to go anywhere. We can just watch TV and read or something. Can I get you a beer?"

He was already headed for the kitchen. Idly, Juliet watched him go, and her eyes were on his long legs, and to her surprise, a very nice butt. Not just okay. Not just nice—spectacular. Which went along with everything else about him, really. She loved the glossy length of his hair, the darkness of his eyes, the—

She thought of all the phone messages from Scott and felt triply guilty. "I don't know if I should," she said in response to his offer of a beer.

Josh grinned at her over the door to the fridge. "It's not life or death, sweetheart. Just a beer."

"You're right. Sure. I'll have one."

"Excellent." He brought her a dark bottle. "Want a glass?"

"Are you having one?"

"Nope." He illustrated by taking a long swallow directly from the lip of the bottle. "Cheers."

"Cheers." Juliet raised hers and took a sip. "Hmm.

That tastes pretty great, actually." She sank down on the couch. "There's something about the mountains that makes everything taste twenty times better."

He settled in the chair and leaned forward, his hands loosely between his legs. A glitter lit his dark eyes. "Are you one of those people who feel better at high altitudes?"

"I feel better in mountains, absolutely, but doesn't everyone? The air is so fresh and clean. Makes me feel ten thousand times better. Clearheaded or something."

"Not everyone does feel better. A lot of people can't tolerate it at all—they get headaches and upset stomachs, can't sleep. But I had a friend once who wasn't much of a talker, and if you got him up in the mountains, he'd start chattering for all he was worth. It made him feel great."

"I guess I'm more in that category."

"Good." He smiled and lifted his beer again. His eyes were fixed on her face, and was it her imagination or was he looking at her mouth? He didn't look away, as was usual, just kept looking at her so directly.

Finally she said, "What? Do I have something on my face?"

"No." His expression grew more serious. "You just have a good face. I like looking at it."

Not "pretty," not "sexy." *A good face.* "I guess that's okay, then." In the warm lamplight, the hard bones and angles of his face were softened. Enormous dark eyes, that hawkish nose, full lips. "Yours is very strong."

He licked his bottom lip and to her amazement, Juliet felt a tiny shock of desire rush down her spine. It suddenly seemed there was dusky warmth in the room, something almost visible blooming right there in the air between them.

And she had no idea what to do with it, or even if she *wanted* to do something. Or not do something. One part of her brain was thinking, *oh, let's kiss him. Those lips are like cake!*

She could see, in the little way he rubbed his lip with the very tip of his tongue, that he thought of it, too. It wasn't as if he was doing it to cause a reaction, but more out of a meditative state, and that made it all the more alluring. He was so big and sexy and—

Her phone rang. "Sorry," she said. "I had this turned off for a whole day and I really should answer it."

"A whole day," he said with a slightly mocking lift of a brow. "Go for it. Do you want something to eat?" He stood up.

"Sure, anything." She flipped open the phone. "Hello?"

"It's about time," Scott said. "I was worried about you. Is everything okay?"

"The reception is patchy," she said, turning her engagement ring around and around in a circle, wondering what *else* she might end up lying to him about. "Sorry about that. I'm fine, but you may as well know I don't have reception at Desi's."

From the corner of her eye, she noticed Josh straightening in the kitchen, and against her will, she looked at him. His well-shaped legs. The long back clad in a heather-blue T-shirt, his amused, raised eyebrow.

The cell reception in Mariposa was spectacular. The well-to-do skiers who vacationed here insisted upon it.

She shrugged at him.

"I wish you'd check in regularly," Scott said. "You know you haven't been well."

A prickle of something moved over her neck. *You haven't been well.* As if she were a vaporous Victorian, prone to faints. "I'm fine, Scott. But I'll do my best to keep in touch. It's just not that easy." Lies, lies, lies. But she was tired of being fussed over and coddled and *watched.* "How is everything in your world?"

"It's good. As a matter of fact, I have to go to dinner with a client, but I thought I'd try you before I left."

"Okay, thanks. I should go, too. I'm at the house of a friend of my sister's."

"Call me soon, then."

"I will. Take care."

He clicked off, and Juliet looked down at the phone, thinking. When had they stopped saying *I love you?* When had they ever had any passion?

"That's not the happiest expression," Josh said, coming back into the room. "Boyfriend troubles?"

She waved the ring. "Fiancé."

Instead of sitting on the chair, he carried a tray of Vienna sausages, string cheese, crackers and grapes to the coffee table and sat down beside her. He smelled of pine and sunshine. "Not the most elegant stuff around, but you know, I've got to feed a four-year-old."

"I didn't know they still made Vienna sausages."

"I eat Spam, too."

She looked a him. "Really."

"I'm a guy," he said, popping a squishy little sausage into his mouth. "We don't have to eat right."

Juliet found a chuckle rolling up from her chest. "Ah. I'll have to remember that."

He gestured toward the phone. "Now, you were saying…fiancé troubles?"

"I don't know." She sighed. "I'm not sure it's working out, but I don't really know why."

"Sometimes, things aren't right, that's all."

"Right." The crackers were grainy, the cheese in neat, white slices. Her stomach growled. "I don't know how I could be hungry. I ate pancakes for breakfast, all that cake and cookies for lunch with your mom and Glory and now this."

"That's not that much food." He made a masterpiece of layering a two-inch sandwich of crackers and cheese and sausages. "But then you're one of those California girls, aren't you? A spinach leaf for lunch, a grain of brown rice for dinner and all the chardonnay you can drink?"

She dropped her jaw in exaggerated shock. "Ow!" Raising a quick eyebrow, she said, "You must know some of my girlfriends."

"They all come here to ski."

"Of course." His knee was only a few inches from her own, and she poked it with one finger. "But not all of us are Hercules, you know, able to down 12,000 calories a day."

"True." He rubbed his broad chest happily. "It's good to be a guy."

She found her gaze on that big hand, the chest beneath it. His fingernails were clean, flat ovals. At the opening of his Henley, the skin was the brown of good wheat bread, very smooth. Absurdly, richly, she imagined her mouth on that sleek triangle of skin.

Lost in a spell of newborn desire, she raised her eyes and found him looking back at her.

In that second, the thickness bloomed around them again. An atmosphere as humid as a cloud, fragrant with possibility. The only thing in the world for a moment was Josh. The lavishly fringed eyes, his quirky mouth, those giant hands that she'd seen could be so gentle.

He leaned forward and put the crackers down, and carefully brushed his fingers clean. Lacing his hands together, he leaned on his knees, putting his face much closer to hers. "Is it my imagination," he said, "or is there something clicking here between us?"

"Clicking is not the right word," Juliet said quietly. Blooming, maybe. She looked at his mouth, and could not even remember when she had so longed for a kiss. His mouth entirely filled her vision—full lower lip, sharply cut upper. Black whiskers, a few millimeters long, grew around his mouth in a sparse goatee shape, and it occurred to her that he probably didn't grow much beard.

"It isn't your imagination," she said, and swallowed.

"That's what I thought," he said, the voice rumbling out of that deep chest with the depth of a drum. His nostrils flared as he looked at her mouth, at her breasts, which pearled embarrassingly, back to her face, all without touching her. "Probably shouldn't do anything about it, though."

"I'm engaged," she offered.

"So you said." He moved one hand and touched her

diamond, just the ring, then the knuckle right above it. "There's more though. You have something in your past."

Juliet swallowed. "Yes."

"And so do I."

"Oh." She looked at him. "What do you have?" Then she waved a hand. "Never mind. You've given me privacy. I'll give you yours."

"It's all right—mine is pretty common. An ex-wife who is unstable and dramatic and kidnapped my daughter."

"I'm so sorry. That's why you're worried about Glory."

"That's right."

She loved the simple straightforwardness of him, the way he met her eyes, the directness of his speech. He was real in a way she hadn't encountered in a long time. In L.A., everybody seemed to feel a need to play to the audience. Not this one.

Honestly, what was this? This narcotic spell he cast? Would he kiss her? Would she let him?

"I can be strong, Princess," he said, "but not if you keep looking at me like that."

"Sorry." With effort, she stood up and walked away. Shaking her head, she turned, donning her lawyer self. "Let's just not do that. Too much going on."

"Agreed. Come eat your crackers and cheese."

She sat back down. "Is it all right if I ask what happened to your ex?"

"It's fine. Nobody knows where she is." He cleared his throat. "Unfortunately, she's an alcoholic and doesn't seem to want to get help, so she's just out there."

"I'm sorry. That's hard."

"It is. And it's especially hard for Glory, who loves her."

Juliet settled a slice of cheese precisely on a single grainy cracker, and balanced it in her fingers. "I assume she was not an alcoholic when you met her."

"Right."

"So, what did the two of you give each other?" She got ready to bite the cracker. "Was it love or need or—what? Why did you fall in love?"

"Hmm." He gave her a look. "Right for the heart of things, huh?"

She shrugged. "You don't have to answer. I'm just thinking about these things."

"What things?"

"Love things." She took a bite of her sandwich.

"Love things," he repeated, and took a breath, looking into the middle distance. "Andy—my ex—is very beautiful. I was just getting out of the army in Colorado Springs and I met her at a nightclub. She was the most beautiful woman I'd ever seen. Glory looks just like her."

Juliet was surprised to note a ripple of jealousy, which she hoped she was hiding.

Josh went on. "She was Indian—Sioux and Cherokee—and proud of it. She was—" he frowned "—somebody I could bring home to my mom, you know? An Indian woman who wouldn't mind the rez. She was a shawl dancer, and had beaded her own moccasins and—" He rubbed his face. "It seems kind of shallow now, but I thought that's what I *should* want."

She wondered what he wanted when he wasn't following shoulds, but she said only, “Ah. And what did she get from you?”

“I don’t really know.”

Juliet had a lot of experience with people who didn’t particularly know the truth, those who were hiding it, and those who had hidden it from themselves. She smiled gently. “Yes, you do.”

For a moment he looked at her. “Yeah, I guess I do. I offered stability. She’d spent her childhood moving around. She liked the fact that I already had a job lined up here as a tribal cop, that we’d have a whole community she could just plug into.”

“So what happened?”

“It bored her to tears.” He grinned. “This a very slow, quiet place in a lot of ways. She’d spent her whole life in cities, and didn’t know how much she’d hate the way everyone knows your business, all that stuff.”

“I get it.” It was a common enough story. She took a sip of beer, dared herself to ask the other question. “So what do you like about women that you don’t feel you should?”

“Blondes,” he said distinctly. “And lots of cleavage.”

Juliet laughed. “Very original.”

“Not at all.” Rakishly, he raised his beer to her. “To you, Princess.”

Heat ran across her cheekbones and the bridge of her nose. “Thanks.”

“What about you,” he asked. “What do you like that you shouldn’t?”

“Other than being wildly attracted to a man who is not my fiancé, you mean?”

"Wildly, huh?"

A knock came at the door, and Juliet frowned, worried it would awaken Glory from her nap. Josh jumped up and hurried to open it.

Desi stood there, fuming. "You know what he did now?" she said, coming into the room.

Juliet put a finger to her lips. "Glory is asleep, sis."

"Sorry." She made a low growling noise, put her face in her hands. "He's just making me so crazy I can't stand it."

Josh rubbed her shoulder. "What happened, Desi?"

"He agreed to sell the land to a developer. His *half!* What the heck does that mean, his half? He also is threatening to get an injunction to keep me from operating the wolf shelter until the land dispute is settled."

"Did you see him?"

She slumped in the chair, stared at the crackers. "No, he called me. He said it looks bad for his business to have a restraining order, and if I wanted to get nasty, that's what he'd have to do."

"So he hasn't actually done anything about it yet," Juliet said.

"I don't know what he's done." She picked up a piece of cheese, examining it as if she'd found it in the Dumpster instead of on a tray in her best friend's living room. Her face brightened. "But I also heard that there are some other people who aren't too happy with old Claude."

"Gossip," Juliet said. "Always good. Who is it?"

"Kay Turner, the dentist's wife—you saw her this morning—is widely known to have a crush on him.

And she's very put out that he's dating Miss Ski Queen of the World."

"But she's married!"

Desi waggled her eyebrows. "I gather her husband's none too happy with any of it, but what can he do?"

Josh scowled. "This is a mess. I want you to just go home tonight and forget about all of it, okay?"

Looking deflated, Desi nodded. "I will."

"Promise?"

"That's what I'm here for," Juliet said. "To make sure she doesn't do anything rash."

"Good," he said. But he didn't look particularly comforted.

As they were getting ready to leave, he touched her shoulder lightly. "I'll be thinking about what you said."

She met his eyes, conscious of Desi's close interest. "Me, too," she said.

"You guys stay out of town for a day or two, huh?"

Juliet nodded. "Will do."

"I'll be by tomorrow to check on her."

There was nothing else to do. Juliet followed her sister down the sidewalk to the truck, feeling his gaze touching her back, her hair, her neck. When she climbed in the front seat and closed the door, she looked back and saw him still watching, his face sober.

She raised a hand and resolutely turned her face away.

Chapter 7

When they got to the cabin, Desi said, "Let's get some wine and go up to the hot springs. That'll burn off some stress."

"It's getting dark, though."

Desi gave her a half smile. "It's not very far, Juliet. There's a trail the entire way. We have flashlights."

"But what about…animals? Like bears and cougars?"

"We'll bring the dogs. Trust me, this is a wonderful thing, these hot springs at night."

"Okay."

Dusk was closing in as they hiked up the hill, carrying thick towels and flashlights and cans of natural soda Desi fished out of the cupboard. At the clearing where the pool bubbled up, Desi dropped her things and stripped off her shirt, then her jeans, folding them neatly and putting them on a rock nearby.

Juliet had done this before, soaked naked in the hot springs with her sister, but it suddenly seemed unwise. Foolish, even. She stood there, hands at her sides, unable to move. Her eye twitched, once. Twice. The smell of earth and minerals rose up from the water, and in the growing dusk, she could see steam rising from the surface.

"C'mon, silly," Desi said, reaching for the straps on her bra.

"I don't think I can this time," Juliet said. "I feel weird about being naked outside."

Desi didn't say anything for a minute, but Juliet felt her measuring eyes. "It won't hurt anything to leave on our bras and panties if that's easier for you."

"I should have brought a bathing suit," Juliet said. "But Colorado, winter, just didn't think I'd need one."

"No big deal. I'm cold, though, so I'm getting in." She stepped into the pool, then submerged and gave a groan. "Oh that's good. C'mon, girl. Climb in."

Juliet shucked her coat and blouse and jeans, hungry for the feel of the water. For a minute, she wished she could be naked, but she decided to not beat herself up about it just this minute, and climbed in. As the hot, scented water enveloped her limbs, she groaned. "This is fantastic!"

There were ledges at various levels, formed cleverly with flat rocks when they built the pool, and Juliet chose one and leaned back, closing her eyes. "It's like having your own spa," Juliet said.

"It is my own private spa," Desi said. "The good mud pools are by the wolf kennels, but I'll show you those, too."

"I know women who would pay a lot of money for this."

"Oh, trust me, one of the developers who wants the land is a guy who wants to do just that. Put in a spa."

"It would make a fortune, Desi."

"That's not what I'm about."

"Well, of course not, but there's nothing wrong with money, is there?"

"No. I just don't think that every square inch of the earth needs to be developed. It's important to keep some of it wild."

"You're right," Juliet said. "Pass me a soda, will you?"

"Absolutely." Desi snapped it open and handed it across the water.

Juliet took a long, cooling swallow, then settled the can on the edge of the pool and let herself slide down further into the water, tipping her head back to rest it against a grassy pillow so she could gaze up at the sky. It had gone velvety with black night, and the darkness glittered with a million zillion stars. The sight made all of her issues and problems seem very, very small.

Desi asked gently, "What happened to you outside the restaurant this morning, honey?"

Because of the big sky and the uncountable stars, Juliet could answer without too much pain in her chest, "Flashback. They keep happening, and I never quite know what will trigger them."

Desi splashed, sitting up. "Why didn't you tell me?"

"There's nothing to tell, really." Juliet let her arms and hands float in the water, free and loose, as if they were not attached to her at all. "They just kind of show up now and then."

"That must be hell. And what an awful sister I am to need you to take care of me when I should be taking care of you."

Juliet, soft boiled and relaxed, shook her head dreamily. "No, don't worry. My counselor said they'll go away eventually."

"What triggered it today?"

"Maybe the doorway. Or maybe the smell of margaritas. I don't know. It's hard, because then I'm not me, standing there, I'm the me I was that night when I got raped."

"I hate him," Desi said fervently. "I'd like to kill that guy."

"Desi!" Juliet sat up. "That's not who you are."

"Oh, yes it is," she said. "Hurt one of mine, and you are dead." She peered through the dark at her sister. "You don't want to hurt him in revenge?"

"I don't even feel that much for him. I just don't care." It was as if there was a wall around the whole miserable incident. "It's like it happened to somebody on television or something, and I can replay it with the sound turned down, but why would I?"

"You know, it doesn't seem to me that you've ever gotten angry over all of this. If I were you, I'd be furious."

"I'm not."

But as if her body and her mind were expressing different things, Juliet felt her throat close, as if there was a scream lodged inside it and she couldn't seem to get it out. Taking a sip of her mandarin lime soda, she said, "I just wish they would have caught him. I hate it that he got away with it."

"Yeah. And he's probably doing it again."

The idea made Juliet feel sick to her stomach. "Don't even say that."

"Sorry." Desi leaned back and tipped her head toward the sky. "Look at those stars, will you?"

Juliet tipped backward, again, too. Between the shadow arrows of pines, she admired a night sky wholly unlike the one she knew at home. This one was deepest black, with no gray or pink on the horizon, and across it were thousands and thousands of twinkling points of light, tiny pinpricks to glowing planets, close and far. At home she could only see a few.

It made space seem incomprehensibly vast, and by comparison, her own problems seemed very small. "I'm so glad to be here, Des," she commented, and rolled the cool can over her forehead.

"I'm glad, too," Desi said. "I was losing it."

In the soft dark, Juliet asked, "Desi, what happened with you two? You used to be so in love."

Desi sighed. "It was never what you thought it was, Juliet." Her voice sounded unbearably weary. "We just got locked into some dance and we couldn't stop."

"Like Mother and Daddy."

"Yes." She took a sip of her own soda. "It doesn't thrill me to say that, I can tell you, but I pretty much reproduced their relationship to a T. The brainy female scientist and the dashing upstart artist."

"Good grief. I never saw that before."

"You're kidding. I saw it years ago, but as I said, we were locked in this dance, and it was very difficult to get out of it once we started."

Juliet thought of the women she worked with, the sorrow in their haggard faces as they spoke of husbands, boyfriends, brothers. "At least you're done now. Or will be soon."

"I know." She was silent for a long time. "I feel like a fool, Juliet. I really do. I'm smart and well-educated and our parents showed us how destructive this kind of union can be, and yet—I did it anyway. I fell for the myth."

"What myth?"

"Oh, I don't know. The fairy tale, I guess. I'm just so angry with him right now!"

"He's behaving badly, sis. You have a right to be angry."

Desi sat up suddenly. "You know, we should get a car from a junkyard and beat the hell out of it with sledgehammers."

Juliet laughed, envisioning the pair of them in old jeans and tattered flannel shirts swinging sledgehammers to the sound of some twangy music. "Or we could try out for roller derby."

"I'm serious. It would be a lot healthier than pretending you're not absolutely furious."

Juliet said, "I'll think about it."

But she didn't see how swinging a hammer at an inanimate object would help, either. It wouldn't give her back her innocence. Anger wouldn't give her back a sense of courage.

* * *

They got back to the cabin around eight, and not long afterward, Desi got a phone call. The way she started barking questions about blood flow and gashes, it sounded like she was dealing with a wounded animal. As she talked, she was taking out warm clothes—jeans, thick socks, sturdy boots.

Juliet busied herself stoking the fire. There was an art to building a good fire—something Claude had taught her back in the old days when he had been a nice person. This one still had embers, so Juliet layered in some medium-sized sticks and thinner kindling and waited for them to catch before she carefully added two logs about the width of her thigh.

Behind her, Desi barked out, "How long ago?" and then, "Where did you see him?"

Desi had a bellows she'd found at an antique fair once, and Juliet used them to fan the flames, watching as they turned bright yellow and started to crackle.

Desi hung up by snapping her cell phone in half. "I'm going to have to take off for a little while, sis. Emergency."

Juliet rocked back on her heels and rested her hands on her thighs. A slight sense of dis-ease rippled down her spine, but she said, "Okay."

"Are you going to be all right?"

"Desi, I'm thirty-two years old. I think I can handle a few hours by myself."

The elder sister smiled ruefully. "Sorry. Maybe I'm projecting. I'm worried about my own ability to cope. You're doing fine." She dressed in the layers of warm clothes, and put on some boots. She attached her replacement cell phone to a clip on her belt. "If you need me, feel nervous, even just want a little reassurance, don't hesitate to call, all right?"

"I'll be fine, I swear."

"You'll have the dogs here. They're great protectors, but don't get nervous if they bark at something. Every so often, they pick up the wolves howling and go nuts."

Juliet put a hand on Sitting Bull's hindquarters and dug her hands into his long thick fur. He groaned and licked her wrist, then fell back to the floor.

Desi opened a long closet and took out a rifle and a box of what Juliet assumed were shells or bullets or whatever. She frowned. "I thought Josh took the gun away from you."

"Please." The word was droll. "He needed to feel better because he's a cop, but there's no way I'd be out in the woods without a rifle."

"What do you need it for?"

"The emergency is a cougar that's been stalking goats. He got one tonight, and injured two more. The rancher shot it, but it took off and now he's worried. If I'm out there looking at bloody goats, I want to be sure I'm not that cat's next meal."

"Desi! That sounds dangerous."

"I'll be all right." Desi put on her heavy coat and tugged her braid out, flinging it over her shoulder like a rope. Juliet liked the sturdy, capable aura that surrounded her sister, and she wondered how it would feel to know how to stitch up an injured goat or do surgery on a wolf or deliver a colt. "I doubt I'll even see the cat, but if he's injured badly, he might be very dangerous."

"Be careful."

"Always."

After Desi left, Juliet dragged the futon mattress to an open spot in front of the fire, bringing dogs and a book with her. There were things Juliet did not love about her sister's cottage. Taking fast, somewhat chilly baths got on her nerves pretty quickly. She sometimes felt anxious about not using too much power or water and knew Desi eyed her excesses—or at least she felt eyed—with disapproval.

But she *loved* the woodstove. The smell of it, that wispy, smoky, woodsy scent; the flickery warmth of it, the sound of it crackling, popping. Desi kept piles of pillows and blankets around and it was easy to pile them up into drifts, then camp down with a book and a cup of hot chocolate and a good novel and read and read and read.

With the dogs. Which was the other thing she loved about the fire and pillows and reading experience—puddles of dogs surrounding her like a moat. All of them were wolf mixes, of course, dogs Desi had adopted over the years, but they were very different animals nonetheless.

Tecumseh had the best fur, thick and fluffy and white, and he liked to speak in little groans and mutterings that Desi told her were indications of the husky portion of his parentage. He loved cuddling, too, which is why she liked him being on the bed with her. She hugged him like a stuffed animal.

Crazy Horse was a fluffy, nervous mutt with big paws and silky black fur and a head that seemed too big for his body. He startled easily and liked to bark, but charmed Juliet by putting his head down and huddling close to her body for attention.

The beauty of the three was an aloof gray-and-black dog named Sitting Bull. He had burly shoulders and a thick tail, and ears that stood alertly on his elegant wolf's head. He didn't speak much, but he was devoted to Desi and brought her tidbits to share now and again, various massacred small animals. He was clearly the alpha. The other dogs deferred to him. He usually slept a bit to the outside of the pack.

Alone in the cabin, with the fire and the dogs for company, Juliet gazed toward sky visible through the window and at the stars twinkling so far away, and the day leaked back into her mind for review.

The day—Claude and his girlfriend, the confrontation on the street. Helene and Glory. Joshua Mad Calf. She smiled. Speaking of alpha wolves!

The flashback, which had been so violent and intense—maybe one of the worst she'd had so far—replayed, too. She pressed cold fingertips to her twitching left eyelid and tried to think about it calmly. It was just a memory replay, nothing to worry about. Time healed wounds like this, and hers would be healed, too.

But the truth was, the flashbacks seemed to be getting worse, and she wasn't sure quite why. The rape, as these things went, had not been particularly terrible—Juliet had been horrified by some of the stories a few women had told in the group therapy sessions she'd attended. Terrible rapes, involving torture or violence or scarring. By comparison, Juliet's had been a very ordinary rape.

She'd been on a business trip in late winter. That was part of the irony, of course. For months, she'd been going to a grim neighborhood in Long Beach to work for the immigrant center, and had never even been frightened.

The business trip was to Albuquerque for a deposition on a civil rights case involving illegal immigrants and their employers. The day had been a long one, and Juliet had a slight headache by the time she got back to her hotel. As always, she was staying in an upscale hotel, with above-average security measures, and as always, she paid attention to her surroundings.

But it was such an ordinary night. An ordinary business hotel. An ordinary hotel restaurant and an ordinary sandwich she ate while she read the newspaper and nursed a single glass of red wine. There were quite a lot of family groups in the restaurant itself and she sat at the bar to give them room. A crime drama played on the television in the corner, and there were a handful of other business travelers in the lounge area watching it.

A businessman at the bar, well-dressed with gray at his temples, asked if she minded if he smoked. She apologized but admitted that she did mind. He politely stepped outside. When he came back in, Juliet was devouring a French Dip and he gave her a smile. "It's a gorgeous night out there," he said. "The patio is enclosed, you know, so it's safe."

"Thanks."

She finished her meal and paid for it, and headed for her room. The door to the patio area stood open, and she thought, *what the heck.* She still had a headache. Maybe she needed a little fresh air.

It was dark, but there were lights around the pool, and a couple sat at one end of the area, so she felt safe enough. She'd just walk once around the pool, then go back upstairs and take a hot bath.

She was nearly back at the starting point when someone grabbed her from behind, one hand slapping around her mouth and the other around her waist. She had time to make a soft ulping sound before her attacker dragged her backward into a dark copse of trees. A branch scraped across her arm painfully, and his hand was cutting hard into her mouth and she couldn't quite figure out what was going on.

At first, she thought, "this is probably not as bad as I think."

He was not a big man, but he was strong. "Don't say a word and it will go smooth and easy. If you make a single sound, I'll hurt you."

Terror bloomed in her chest, spread through her limbs, making her feel weak.

She could only whimper softly. He mancuvered her to the ground, shoved a handkerchief into her mouth, and unzipped her dress. She froze.

It was going to happen. He was going to *rape* her.

She began to shiver violently, uncontrollably, and he shook her, once. "Stop that! I won't hurt you if you just cooperate."

Her dress fell down her arms, and he did something—she later found out he cut it—so her bra fell off. The night air struck her exposed skin, his hands clutched her breasts, and she nearly gagged, feeling physically sick at the invasive touch of this stranger.

Tears dripped down her face. Shame. She squeezed her eyes tight against it.

"Stop crying," he growled, and jerked her into place. "I hate that."

But however much he hated it, she couldn't stop, not the crying or the shivering. She shivered as he ripped off her panties and shoved himself into her. It hurt. It took forever and it made him mad. He shoved her this way and that, hands grabbing, groping, twisting.

Bizarrely, she heard the sound of diners just a stone's throw away, the clatter of silver against plates. The smell of margaritas and cigarettes filled her nostrils. He finally finished, and she wept harder in relief and in more fear—would he do it again? Would he kill her?

He pushed her down to the ground facefirst and picked up her clothes. He hit her once, very hard, and she didn't move for a minute, terrified he would do it again. His footsteps disappeared almost eerily fast.

She lay there, stunned, for an indeterminate amount of time, then slowly she moved one arm. It functioned normally and she spread it out, looking for something to cover her nakedness. She found her dress, but everything else was gone, including her shoes.

There was no help for it. She shook out the dress, tugged it over her head then stood there a moment, trying to get her bearings. She felt light-headed and strange, as if she'd run too long on the treadmill or something, but some still-coherent lawyer part of her brain insisted she look around for anything that might be a clue. She tried to figure out how to mark this exact spot, and finally broke a branch and stuck it in the ground where the grass was already springing back around the imprint of her body.

That done, she made her way out of the trees and looked for the couple that had been sitting at the end of the swimming pool. They were gone. In dismay, she had to go back into the doorway she'd come out of, and go back into the restaurant.

The bartender took one look at her, and picked up the phone. "Get the police here," he barked, then slammed the phone down, came around the bar, and managed to snag Juliet and lead her to a chair before she fell down.

"Breathe, honey," he said. "You're all right now."

She bent over and put her head to her knees. Then it came to her that she must look frightening, her hair mussed and shoes off, and she didn't want the children in the restaurant to be frightened. "Maybe," she said, straightening slightly, "I should just go in the other room, out of sight?"

"I can take you to the office," he said. "Lean on me."

So they went to the restaurant office and someone brought her a drink of water.

By the book, she thought now, running her fingers through Tecumseh's thick fur. She'd done absolutely everything by the book. The police came and took her to the hospital to be examined, evidence collected. As these things went, she had escaped without much damage. Some bruising. A black eye and a split lip, and scrapes down the front of her body. The nurse tended her gently, directed her to a rape counselor.

Juliet had attended the counseling sessions, including the group sessions her therapist recommended. She talked it out with people she trusted, cried and got it out like that. She even escaped the looming specter of HIV and STDs and could finally move on with her life.

Or so she thought.

It was little things that went wrong. She couldn't remember things very well, like where she parked her car or what time an important meeting was. She dropped the ball in court one day when a man reminded her of the businessman in the restaurant that night.

She couldn't sleep at night and couldn't stay awake in the daytime. She didn't want to have sex, and at first, Scott was patient, but he understandably grew frustrated as time went by. In sympathy, she finally gave in. It wasn't traumatic, she didn't *mind* it, particularly, but she didn't feel anything, either.

Maybe she never would. Sometimes it felt like something was broken inside of her when she was raped. Some unnamable part, an invisible spiritual limb that now lay in shards, jamming up the emotional works.

As if he sensed her distress, Crazy Horse sighed and snuggled closer. Juliet clasped his furry warmth and buried her face in his warm fur and wondered what it would be like to be a wolf in a pack.

Safe, she thought. Safe and warm.

Chapter 8

At 4:21 a.m., Josh's cell phone rang. "Joshua Mad Calf," he said gruffly.

"Josh, we found a body." It was his boss, Dave Jiramillo, on the reservation. "You need to get down here."

"Body?" Josh croaked. "What body? Dead of what?"

"Not sure yet. There's some mauling, but we're not sure if it's the cause of death. Looks like he's been shot."

"What?" Josh swore. "Murdered, you mean?"

"Looks like it."

Before he could help himself, Josh swore again. He put his head down into the pillows, listening to directions to the location, his heart thudding heavily in his chest. Unease. Warning. This was not going to be good, he could feel it.

"An animal's been at him," Dave said, "so it's not a particularly pretty crime scene."

"I'll be there as soon as I can."

He dressed, called his mother to let her know he'd be bringing Glory over, then wrapped up his sleepy-headed child into a thick blanket and carried her two blocks. The moon was high over the Mariposa ridge, spilling cold light down the grassy slopes, illuminating the ghostly quiet of the middle of the night. No one was about but a pair of dogs ambling down the empty streets. In the distance, an owl hooted.

Appropriate.

His mother was waiting, bundled in her robe. She pushed the screen door open and Josh carried Glory into the room she used there, made sure she was settled, and went back to the main room. "I don't have time to talk," he said in a quiet voice, kissing her forehead, "but they found a body up on the reservation, and I've gotta go check it out."

Helene took a breath and crossed herself, half-Catholic after all these years. "Go," she said.

With dread, he pulled his hat close down on his head and headed out, a bad feeling sitting hard in his gut. The reservation started at the edge of Mariposa, forming the western border of the town and stretching for 1900 square miles into the San Juan mountains, inhospitable and difficult country that was too steep for farming or most ranching. There were no passes through the mountains, not even many jeep tracks. Until a few years ago, the people had been distributed in seven very poor villages that based their livelihood in sheep farming, wool, and loaning out bodies to the hotel and ski industries during the winter months. For most of the twentieth century, it had been one of the poorest reservations within U.S. borders.

Then gambling swept through the Indian nations, one after the other, and the Mariposa Utes had finally approved the measure. They raised capital through elections and by leasing several hundred acres of prime land to developers, and built the casino. It had been wildly successful. The nation was no longer poor.

Crime had increased, but not dramatically, and certain crimes—namely Indian on Indian—had even decreased.

Murder on the rez, and even in Mariposa, was not unheard of, but it was rare. A few years ago, there had been a dramatic family crime—two teens killing their parents and two friends—and there were the usual spousal murders. Josh couldn't think of a time he'd ever been called to an outdoor crime scene with a murdered body.

This one was not far into the rez, only a couple of miles from town, a field bordered by public forest and open grazing. When Josh arrived, the area had been secured with yellow police tape, and a police cruiser from Mariposa had come in with floodlights to illuminate it enough for an investigation, but even given the drama, there were not many people there—a few deputies, the coroner, the Mariposa county hard crimes detective, and two tribal officers. They were all waiting, respectfully, for Josh to arrive. He settled his hat and stepped out, slamming the door smartly.

He didn't like dead bodies much. He'd done his time

as an MP in the first Gulf War and had witnessed enough violent death there to see him through to the end of his own days. It was the biggest reason he'd chosen to come back home to the reservation rather than take a job in the cities.

But even out here, there was sometimes something ugly. This scene, for instance. Stark white light blistered the body into sharp black and white lines. It sprawled facedown in a sloppy patch of mud, the clothes shredded along the upper back and around the shoulders. Josh could see a long braid, but out here, that could be male or female, though this body looked male.

"Do we have an ID?" Josh asked.

"'Fraid so," the deputy said, a stout young woman with high red cheekbones. "Claude Tsosie, a Navajo enrolled on the tribal rolls at Tuba City. He's been shot, in the chest."

Claude.

Josh shook his head, the sense of dread doubling, tripling. "Estimated time of death?"

"Coroner thinks maybe about 10:00 p.m."

"And who found the body?"

"Paul Martinez, over there. He was walking home from his girlfriend's house and saw the white of the shirt."

Josh nodded. "Who have we talked to?"

"Nobody yet."

"All right." Josh stepped in to take a better look. His training, cold and analytical, kicked in as he took notes and barked out orders and collected evidence, but a little voice in his head prayed silently: *please let Desi have a good alibi.*

* * *

Juliet awakened to the sound of her cell phone ringing Alicia Keys' song about "a real man," her signal that it was Scott calling in. Jolted guiltily out of sleep, she pushed the dog off of her and scrambled in her socks to the counter, where her purse sat, and managed to snare the phone before it stopped ringing.

"Hello?" she said breathlessly.

"Hi, Juliet," Scott said. "Did I wake you?"

It was freezing in the cabin and Juliet scurried back to her piles of pillows and blankets and dogs. "I guess you did. What time is it?"

"Eight here, so nine there."

"Wow." She looked over her shoulder—Desi was already gone. "My sister must have just let me sleep."

"So, you're at the cabin? I thought you didn't have reception there?"

Wincing at how very quickly her lie had come back to haunt her, Juliet said, "You know how it is with cell phone reception. Sometimes it's great, sometimes horrible. Maybe it's a very clear day."

"Well, at any rate," he said, "I'm glad to finally be able to talk to you. I miss you."

Juliet plucked at the yarn used to quilt the enormous blanket over her legs, emptiness crashing through her. "Me, too."

"You must be getting some excellent rest."

"I really am. Desi and I got a lot done yesterday, too—restraining order and some legal paperwork filed."

"Good. I know you've been worried about her."

"How are things with you? Tell me about the Whiting case."

She made small talk with him, pretending it all mattered somehow. Once it had. She tried hard to call up his face, his eyes, his hands. Nothing seemed real. He seemed like a character in a book she'd read a long time ago, thin and vague.

As he talked, she could feel how hard he was working to keep her attention, and a clear, sudden recognition settled on her: it was not fair to keep this up, this masquerade of the Juliet Who Felt Something. Breaking up hurt, but not as much as lies.

But how to begin?

When a slight lull fell between them, she said quietly, "You know, Scott, I've been thinking I might not be coming back there." The words ran like electric shocks down her nerves, rippling down her spine and arms—surprise. "To Los Angeles."

It stunned them both. A long silence, filled with the implications of what she'd just said, fell.

"You're going to live in Mariposa?" he asked finally, his voice thin. "Why would you do that?"

"I just don't think I want to live in L.A. anymore. I don't want that job or that life or—anything."

"Or me?" his voice sounded hollow, like an empty restaurant.

"It's not you, Scott," she said, knowing it was a cliché even though she meant it. In the middle of her chest was a dull burn, a recognition of the pain she was causing him, but even as she rubbed the heat of it, her shoulders suddenly didn't feel as hunched. "I just don't know what I feel anymore and it's not fair to you to keep you hanging on this way."

"But we're engaged!"

"I know." She rolled her shoulders. "I think it's time that we are not." She paused. "Engaged. Anymore."

"This seems rash," he said.

"It's not rash, and you know it if you're honest with yourself."

"Juliet, it's been a little weird the past few months or so, but you've had a hard time, and you probably shouldn't make any big decisions."

"Scott, I want you to be free to date other people. I have no idea when I'm going to get my head together."

"I don't want anyone else."

Juliet took a breath. "Scott, I'm so sorry, but I can't see you anymore."

"Don't do this," he said, blustering. "You can't do this to me!"

"*To* you? I'm doing it *for* you!"

"I've been here for you. I've been really patient."

"You have."

At the other end of the line, he sighed. "You're really doing it aren't you?"

"I really am. I'm sorry."

"Stop saying that, like I'm some pity case or something. You're the one who needs pity, not me!"

He hung up on her.

Juliet fell backward. "That went well," she said to Tecumseh, scratching his head. "Maybe we need to get some coffee."

The phone rang in her hand. Scott's number came up

on the screen and she hesitated. Maybe she should just be done with it. And yet, what if the situation was reversed—wouldn't she want to have her say? She flipped the phone open. "Hi, Scott."

"I'm sorry. I lost my temper."

"It's okay. But let's not do this, okay, the back and forthing. I'm really breaking up with you and there isn't anything you can say to change my mind." She almost added, *I'm sorry,* but remembered in time that it had upset him.

"Just let me ask this one thing," Scott said. "Have you met somebody?"

Unbidden came Josh's face, the harsh slash of cheekbone and jaw, the licorice black of his hair. Guilt, the color of bile, burst through her. "No," she said.

"Will you do me one favor then?"

"If I can."

"Give it a little time. Don't give up on all of this until you've had time to heal."

Juliet bowed her head. "I can't do that favor, Scott. This is final." She breathed the phrase anyway. "I'm sorry," she said, and hung up.

Coffee. Definitely coffee was in order. She slid into a pair of jeans and tugged wool socks over her toes, let the dogs out, and padded into the kitchen. There was no automatic coffeemaker, of course, only an aluminum percolator you put on the stove and boiled the old-fashioned way. Juliet liked it quite a bit, loved the crystal percolator button on top, and the sound of it bubbling up, like an old television commercial, and the smell filling the kitchen like some heady cologne.

Sunlight streamed in through the window by the sink, and the bars of yellow light falling over the polished pine framing gave the moment a depth of serenity Juliet found surprising. She crossed her arms, leaned a hip against the counter, and wondered what it was that made it seem so lovely. Through the window, she could see pines and blue sky and the jagged line of mountain rising high.

She felt lighter than she had in months. How could she have not realized how much she wanted to break up with Scott, all this time? What else was in her life that she wanted to let go?

She called up her life, and really, there wasn't much to it, was there? Scott, her condo, her job. Essentially, the job was gone, and she'd known it the minute she'd lost what should have been an easy win. The lives at stake were too important to risk on a sloppy lawyer, which was what she'd become over the past year, sadly enough.

In time, she'd be ready to go back to work. When she had her head together. When she could think about a courtroom without thinking of her rapist being on trial.

She liked working for the people, trying to even things out between the little guy and government or business, but a person could do that in many different ways.

She might miss her friends, but this wasn't her first big move. *If* it ended up being a move. Which left the condo in old Hollywood, her pride and joy, with all its Art Deco touches and glowing woods. It was a beauty, with a fireplace, within walking distance of shopping and restaurants and the bus line. She'd paid a pretty penny for it, but the value had nearly doubled since then. If she sold it, could she buy something in Mariposa?

Would she even want to?

Maybe it was better to just stick with the condo for awhile. Not too many changes at once.

Humming under her breath, she poured coffee and thought about how to spend this beautiful day.

Josh drove to Desi's ranch with a heaviness in his gut. Of course it could only be he who delivered the news, and he didn't expect Desi to take it particularly well.

It seemed incongruous to be bringing such bad news on such a great day. Melting snow dripped from the trees, pattering and dazzling on such a bright day. Most of the snow was gone, but he knew there was meant to be more tomorrow afternoon. He made a note to be sure they had plenty of supplies in case of a blizzard.

He parked under his favorite tree and got out. Desi's truck was not in its usual place. He'd hate to have to go find her at work to deliver this news, and had tried to get here a little sooner, for precisely this reason. Reluctantly, he crossed the gravel, steering clear of a puddle. Three dogs came running through the trees, barking first in warning, then in welcome when they saw who it was.

He knocked on the door. In seconds, Juliet swung it open, and Josh was awash, once again, with the luscious, somehow innocent sensuality of her. Her pale hair was slightly mussed, as if it had not yet been brushed, and her face was absolutely bare of makeup, showing pale smooth skin only lightly freckled across the nose. She wore a flowered Henley with three buttons and long sleeves and no bra, which he tried mightily not to notice, but there was such a delicious loose sway of breasts beneath thin cotton that he couldn't help it. Her feet were bare.

"Hi, Josh."

"Hi," he said, and cleared his throat. "Is Desi here?"

"I think she went to work already. Do you want to come in?"

"Um." He tried to think. The smell of coffee blasted out of the kitchen, thick as a giant arm snaring him around the neck. "God, that smells good. Yeah, I'd love some of that coffee."

She moved away from the door, leaving it open for him to come in.

As he entered, he saw the pile of covers and pillows before the fire, still rumpled from her sleep, and damned if he didn't feel a little heat in his sex, a wash of awareness over his lower belly, a wish to have her back in those mussed covers, naked, with him on top of her. Kissing. Bare-chested, bare-hipped, legs tangling—

"Cream and sugar?" Juliet asked.

"What?" He blinked, aware of a graininess behind his eyes, in his throat. It had been a long night. "Yes, please."

"You don't look very well, Josh," she said. "Come sit down. Is there something wrong?"

He settled on a bar stool. "Long night," he said, reluctant to go into it just yet.

"This will help." She came around the counter and

put the cup down beside him, then rested her hand on his shoulder. "Can I get you something to eat? There are eggs, some bread."

Up close, he smelled her skin, something vaguely meadowlike, the slightest bit spicy, like crushed grasses. He found himself noticing the hollow of her throat, the rise of collarbones on either side, her breasts, with raised nipples burning through the cloth. He felt dizzy with the desire to touch her, weigh her breasts in his palms, taste her mouth, feel her body close to his own.

With a sense of near-despair, he wanted more than anything to just be held, and it shamed him.

"It must have been terrible," she said. Her voice was smooth and deep, like a hot spring pool, and her hand moved on his hair, as if she petted a dog.

He bent his head, trying to maintain a sense of propriety. Her hand moved on his neck, smoothing the skin over the tense muscles there, and he felt the touch through his whole body.

Josh lifted his head, and Juliet swayed forward and pressed a kiss to his brow, put her hands on his face. "What can I do?" she asked, and there was her pricelessly pretty face, so scrubbed and lovely, and he put his hand up around her neck and pulled her closer, between his knees. Her breasts touched his upper chest, surprisingly full and soft, and their eyes locked for a long, long second, hers smoky and sure and vibrantly blue. Her fingers were cool, almost cold. He put his hands on the small of her back, nudged her closer, and lifted his face to receive the kiss she bent down to offer.

It was one of those moments that would not come

again, and Josh tried to gather as many details as he could. The sway of her back beneath his palms, the smell of her skin, the cold tips of her fingers against his cheekbones.

The very good taste of her mouth. A good mouth. Plump lips, breath that tasted of sugar, a sweetness he expected and a heat he hadn't. He let her lead, let her just do whatever it was she was doing here. One moist kiss, two. His chest ached and he wanted to pull her more closely against him, but something told him not to.

But it was funny how it seemed there was light flowing between them. Not just nerves and excitement and arousal, but actual light, as if her lips flipped on some switch inside of him.

She raised her head. Her thumbs moved on his jaw, sweeping lightly against the bone. "Did that help any?"

"What about your fiancé?"

She pulled a hand from his face and showed him the bare space on her left hand. "We broke up. This morning."

"I'm glad," he said, and meant it.

"Me, too." She stepped away. "Let me get you some coffee and eggs."

"I need to—uh, tell you something, Juliet. This morning—" His voice, always gravelly, gave out on him. He cleared his throat. "I have something else to talk about. The reason I came here."

"Okay." Trouble came over her eyes, clouding the vivid blue. She stepped out of his embrace. "What is it?"

"First, do you know where Desi is?"

"She must have gotten up early. I haven't been up

that long, really." She glanced over her shoulder at the bed. "Why?" she said suddenly in alarm. "Is she hurt or is there an accident or—"

"No, she's not hurt. When was the last time you saw her?"

"Last night. She was called out to an animal emergency and I went to bed."

Josh's belly dropped. "What time was that, do you remember?"

A quick shrug. "I don't know. About nine, maybe?"

Mentally, he swore. This would not look good for her at all. It might not *be* good. He had to remember to think like a cop, not like Desi's buddy. What if she had killed him? "And you haven't seen her since?"

"*No.* I already said that. You're scaring me, Josh. What happened?"

He squared his shoulders. "Claude is dead, Juliet. We found his body out on the rez last night."

Her hand flew to her mouth. "Dead? How? Like murdered? Or in a car accident or something?"

"We're waiting for the autopsy, but it's pretty clear he was shot to death."

Juliet went so white he was afraid she'd faint. Carefully, she sank down to a stool, and let go of a breath. "Do you have ideas who did it?"

"Not yet."

She raised her eyes. "It's not Desi, you know. She might seem as if she'd like to kill him, but I know she wouldn't really do it."

"I know that, too," he said, and realized it was true. He could see her shooting Claude during a confrontation, but not stalking him to shoot him dead, or luring him out to some deserted place. "But it's not going to look good for her, not after that run-in yesterday in front of half the town."

Juliet pressed her lips together. "Damn."

"And the trouble is, she has the most motive. Who would blame her for killing him?"

"Right," Juliet said grimly, and looked at him hard. "I hear what you're saying, but there's no way she did it." She rubbed her palms on her jeans. "Do you know the land is worth ten million dollars?"

He whistled. "There's motive."

"Talk that one up," she said, and he suddenly realized he wasn't dealing with soft Juliet, but a tough lawyer who probably did very well in court, thank you very much. "Let me find my cell and I'll try to call her."

"I already tried," he said. A headache throbbed at the back of his skull, low, right over his neck. "No answer."

"We need to find her."

Josh nodded and then asked the question he had to ask. "Are you sure she even came home last night?"

Chapter 9

Juliet darted a glance at the bed. What she had not noticed upon awakening was the yellow sweater, inside out and sleeves akimbo, that Desi had flung there last night. Juliet remembered her tugging it off over her head, her hair coming loose in a heavy tumble.

"Maybe she wasn't here last night," Juliet admitted.

"Did she tell you anything about the call?"

"Yes." Juliet frowned. "Goats. Some goats were attacked by a mountain lion. She had to take—" Another wave of guilt swamped her and she halted, the salty taste in her mouth.

"Had to take what?"

"Her rifle. For protection."

Josh pursed his lips. "It's not surprising, considering." He dropped his head in his hands. So weary.

Juliet didn't know if she should comfort him or protest or weep. She crossed her arms over her chest and waited.

He raised his head. "What do you remember about the call? Do you think it was really an animal call?"

She thought back. "We'd just gotten out of the hot springs, you know. I was tired and not paying much attention." She narrowed her eyes, trying to recreate the moment in her mind from the things she could remember. The yellow sweater. The fire in the grate. The sound of Desi's voice, murmuring, pausing.

Where did you see him?

In a split second, Juliet chose her sister over any other thing, even the truth. "I'm absolutely sure," she said.

"All right." He pulled his cell phone off his belt and punched in a number. "Let's find out who keeps goats."

The only possibilities, according to the main vet office, were Alvin Taylor, Pauline Two Tree and John Crum. The first was a wealthy rancher, sitting on about fifty million dollars in land in a flat strip between the two mountain ranges. He turned out to be on an extended vacation and his ranch manager didn't have a record of anything happening to goats the night before. They had, however, seen the mountain lion several times in the past few weeks.

Two Tree lived on the edge of the reservation. Her goats, used for their hair in her weaving, were fine, as carefully tended as small children.

Which left Crum, an ex-hippie turned farmer on the outskirts of town. Josh turned in to his drive and a dozen creatures skittered out to see who had arrived—dogs, goats, a couple of sheep. Chickens squawked and chuttered from their coop, protected from prey behind two layers of fencing.

"A mountain lion would have a good time here, all right," Josh said.

"Poor things."

He gave a little shrug. "It's just nature."

A man with a beard combed neatly to his waist came out of the house carrying a rifle. He wore jeans and a cowboy hat and heavy work boots. Juliet wanted to laugh—he looked like a cartoon version of a mountain man. "I didn't think people like him still existed," she said quietly before they got out.

"Don't you dare make me laugh," Josh said with a glance.

"I'll do my best."

They got out of the truck and Juliet held out her hand for a big shaggy dog to sniff. The man stood there suspiciously. "Can I help you folks with something?"

"We're looking for Dr. Rousseau, the vet? Her office thought she might have come here last night," Josh said.

"Yeah, she was here, but I ain't seen her since she stitched up the goats."

"Do you remember what time that was, sir?"

"Must been ten, ten-thirty, I guess. I just missed the news."

Juliet felt a sense of mingled dread and relief. Relief that Desi actually had been called out to tend some wounded animals, dread that she had been out all night. "Did she say anything about what she was planning to do when she left here?"

"Yup." He lifted his hat, pulled it down tighter over

his ears. "She was gonna go track that blasted cougar while the tracks were fresh."

"Damn," Josh muttered under his breath. Then, more loudly, "Where?"

"She headed out to the reservation. Said she thought she might know where it had its den."

"By the reservation," Josh repeated dully.

The man hawked and spit. "Wasn't that she wanted to kill it, you know. I shot it. She was afraid it might be dangerous."

"All right." Josh held out his hand. "Thank you."

For a moment, the man just stood there, then abruptly stuck out his hand and stiffly shook Josh's. "I gotta protect my critters."

"I understand, sir. A rogue cat can take down a lot of livestock." He tipped his hat. "Take care now."

Back in the truck, Juliet put her hands in her lap, clasped tightly together, and started straight ahead.

"I'm scared," she said, and looked at Josh. "Where is she?"

His mouth could never look tight, but there was grimness to it. He shook his head slowly. "We found the body out there. It was mauled by a big animal. Could have been a cat."

"Maybe somebody shot him accidentally, aiming for the cat?"

"Sure, I mean, it's possible." He seemed to notice her fear and reached across the seat to take her hand. "We'll find her. There's a perfectly reasonable explanation she's missing. Keep the faith."

She nodded.

"Try her cell phone again."

"Good idea." Juliet pulled the phone out of her pocket, jabbed the speed dial. It rang once, then again. Again. Again. The answering machine picked up, and Juliet left a message. "I'm getting seriously worried, Desi. Call me." She hung up and looked at Josh. "Now what?"

"I'll take you home."

The phone rang shrilly and Juliet answered urgently. "Hello?"

"Juliet," Desi cried, "Where are you? It freaked me out to get home and find you gone."

"Where am *I?* Where are *you?* I've been worried to death about you."

"I'm fine. Are you in town? Where did you go?"

It suddenly occurred to Juliet that her sister did not yet know the news, of course, that she was still living in a world where Claude Tsosie was a pain in the neck, but still alive. "I'm with Josh," she said. "We're on our way back there. Don't go anywhere, okay?"

"No way. I chased that lion halfway around the world last night."

"Did you get him?"

"No." She sighed, and Juliet could imagine her rubbing her hand across the back of her neck, a gesture she'd repeated at moments of exhaustion since childhood. "He's wounded, and likely very dangerous, and I'm really worried that he could be a problem. I want to get some wildlife officials out there to sedate him and bring him down so we can fix him up."

"Will they do that?"

"I don't know. We'll see."

"I'll be there soon, sis."

Josh held out his hand for the phone. Juliet handed it to him, and he spoke to Desi. "I'm beat, Desi. Make some coffee, will you?"

Juliet couldn't hear her sister's reply, but Josh clipped the phone closed and handed it back to her.

"Listen," Josh said, "I know this is kind of weird, that life is all in a tangle, but before we go in there and face the way your sister is going to feel about her ex getting murdered, I'd like to know if that kiss this morning means maybe we can figure out a way to see each other. Sometime. Soon."

"It is kind of weird," she said. "But, yeah, I'd like that, too."

He smiled. "Have I told you I have a weakness for blondes?"

"That's because we are princesses," she said, and promptly felt guilty. But there was something about him that made her want to just stop struggling, stop building up defenses, and just rest with him. "I mean, of course there are brunette princesses as well—"

He laughed, the sound as rich as coffee, as chocolate, all things dark and tasty. "Now you know what kind of trouble I get into liking blondes. It's *so* politically incorrect."

Juliet laughed softly and as it rolled out of her chest, she realized it had been a long time since she'd heard it, her own laughter. How odd that it should arrive now, when there had been a murder, when she was dreading the look on her sister's face when she heard her ex was dead.

And yet, why not? Something about this gentle giant

eased her, and she'd been tense so long she was starved for that simple pleasure.

"I won't be able to leave Desi today," she said. "Let's play it all by ear."

"Maybe Glory and I can make supper for you one night. How about that?"

"I'd like that." Juliet smiled. "Glory. What a kid. How did she get that name?"

His nose wiggled in amusement. "My ex liked the song, 'Angels We Have Heard On High.'"

She laughed.

"She was a little strange," Josh acknowledged, "even before she started drinking."

"Glory is a pretty name, and it suits her. She's such a glorious little girl."

"She is."

They stopped at a traffic light. "Her kidnapping…that had to be pretty hard for you."

He touched his nose with the pad of his thumb. "It was brutal. Every single minute." He shook his head. "Who knows what it was like for her?"

"She seems all right, though."

"So far so good. She's with me now, and that's the important thing."

A vision of Desi's face crossed Juliet's imagination, and she pressed a palm to her belly. "I'm so worried about how Desi will take this news. She really did love him, at least she did at one time. I think it's going to break her heart."

"I'm a lot more worried that she might be arrested for it."

"Arrested!"

"Yeah. She has no alibi, and there really aren't many leads at the moment."

Feeling airless, Juliet pressed harder against her stomach. "That would be *so* bad."

"I agree." He cleared his throat. "Let's not cross that bridge just yet. One thing at a time."

"All right." Fingering her phone, Juliet said, "I guess I'm going to have to call my other sister, let her know what's going on. She gets very upset if she gets left out of the loop."

"The artist sister, right?"

"Yes, Miranda. She lives in New York."

He turned on the road toward the cabin. "Shakespeare, huh? Miranda, Juliet and—what's Desi short for?"

"Desdemona."

"Ah." As if he sensed her nervousness, he said, "Is Miranda older, younger?"

"Youngest. The redhead. There's a blonde, a brunette and a redhead. She's the fiery one. More the child of our parents than we are, really." The truck rocked over a deep rut, and Juliet grabbed the door. "Not that she ever sees them. I get the impression that she does everything she can to distance herself from them."

"It's not like you and Desi are living in the old family home, producing grandchildren."

"That's true." Juliet thought of her mother, Carol, her long dark hair and piercing eyes, and felt a pang. "They weren't the best parents. And probably Miranda got the worst of it. They went through some drama when she was in high school. I've never really heard the whole story, but it wasn't pretty for her." She glanced at him. "Sorry, I'm babbling."

"It's interesting. Desi doesn't talk about your family, except you."

"We were pretty close as kids. She was the brave one and I was the coward."

He grinned. "I don't believe that."

"Trust me, it was true. I was afraid of everything—snakes, spiders, all the outside stuff. Desi never was." The cabin came into view. "Oh, dear. Here we go."

They pulled into the circular drive and Juliet couldn't help but think about the first day she'd come here, when Claude had been trying to coax Desi into seeing things his way, and she'd been promising to kill him if he took another step.

What if Desi really had done it? Killed Claude?

No. Juliet set her jaw and got out of the truck. No, she wouldn't allow that possibility. As they came in, she called out, "Hello! Anybody here?"

Desi sat by the potbellied stove, drying her hair. "Just us elves."

Juliet paused, letting one more placid moment pass in Desi's world before they shattered it. Desi sat on the floor, on a pink and paisley cushion. Sitting Bull, glum as ever, sat beside her. Desi's hair, her glory, fell in splendid lushness over her shoulders and down her back. Juliet forgot, because Desi kept it braided, how beautiful her sister's hair was. Yards of it, deep brown like earth or bark, shot through with gold and threads of copper. It flowed down her back like the hair of some medieval queen.

"Desi," Juliet said. "I have some bad news."

Something in Juliet's voice must have conveyed the depth of the bad news, because Desi put down the brush and looked up. There was a scratch on her cheek and marks on her forearms. Pale blue bruises ringed her eyes.

"Well, don't just stand there," she snapped. "*Tell* me!"

Behind Juliet, Josh tensed, as if waiting, and the lawyer in Juliet knew he was probably going into cop mode. What would Desi do? How would she react?

Juliet sank down on her knees. "Claude is dead."

"What?" Desi sounded irritated, impatient.

"Claude is dead," Juliet repeated. "I'm sorry."

For a long moment, Desi waited, as if for the punch line, some other words to change the reality of what Juliet said. Her brown eyes, luminous as the moon, searched her sister's face. "He's dead?"

"Yes." Juliet felt relief rippling through her at Desi's bewilderment.

"Which means what, exactly? Does that pseudo-sale go through and I lose half the land?"

"I don't know. Desi, what does that matter right now? He's dead."

"I heard you." Suddenly, she crumbled forward. "How? Car accident?"

"Murdered," Josh said, that grizzly bear voice making the word even more harrowing.

Desi's head jerked up. "*Murdered?* That's impossible. Who would kill him? I mean, aside from me, of course."

"Don't even joke about it," Juliet cried.

"I wouldn't really kill him. You know that." Desi jumped up. "What happened?"

"He was shot," Josh said. "Last night some time. Found his body on the reservation."

Desi's jaw went hard as she looked at her friend. "Last night," she repeated. "How did he die?"

"Shot," Josh repeated patiently, understanding Desi's shocked and disconnected reaction.

"Damn," Desi whispered. "This is not good for our team at all, is it?"

Grimly, he shook his head. "Half the town heard you tell him you'd kill him."

She took a breath. "Well, then you'd better get out there and find out who really did it. I'll be damned if he ruins my life, that bastard." She shook her head. "What a lousy day." She bent her head and started to cry. "That poor cat is still out there in agony and I'm worried sick that he's going to hurt someone."

Juliet sank down beside her sister, putting her arms around her and whispering, "Shh. It's okay. You'll be all right."

"Find out who killed him, Josh," Desi said.

"I will," Josh said. "I promise."

The skies were getting heavy by midafternoon, when Desi came in from tending her wolves. "I think it's going to snow for real tonight," she said, shedding her down coat and hanging it on a hook. "We have plenty of food, but do you have enough reading material?"

Juliet looked up from the paperback she was reading, curled up in a nook by the windows, Crazy Horse the dog beneath her knees, like a furry pillow. She scratched his forehead idly as she read, nibbling little foods like pistachio nuts and small candies, as she had all her life. Reading and nibbling were always her favorite things. As a child, she'd sometimes read a book a day, happily inert in some corner. In those days, it had usually been a cat who curled up with her.

"Very funny," Juliet said, because they'd bought a paper bag full of novels at a used bookstore the day before. "I think I'll live."

Desi smiled, and it lightened the dark circles beneath her eyes, though there was only so much to be done. "Let's make some cookies, shall we?"

"Definitely an excellent idea." Juliet yawned and put her book down. Crazy Horse groaned and fell to one side. "Did you call Miranda? Let her know what happened?"

"Yes. And Mother and Dad. They're in Greece and send their love." With an exaggerated smooching sound, she kissed the air, then rolled her eyes. "I told them not to interrupt their trip for this. We were divorcing anyway."

Not, Juliet thought cynically, that they would have anyway. They'd never been fond of Claude, which had probably been at least part of his appeal. Desi had never been able to resist needling her mother at every possible chance, a repayment for the endless, endless prodding and poking the eldest daughter had endured from their elegant, blue-blooded mother. She plopped down on the bar stool by the counter and plucked a chocolate chip out of the bag Desi had opened. "What did Miranda have to say? How is she?"

"Fine. I told her you were here and she sent her love." Desi settled a bowl on the counter. "Does she know about the rape? I wasn't sure."

Juliet shook her head. "Can that just be our secret? I hate how people look at me after they find out."

"She's your sister. She won't look at you that way."

"Why burden her with it? There's no point, and it will just upset her."

Desi lifted a shoulder. "What if she'd been raped? Would you want her to tell you?"

With excruciating care, Juliet lined three chocolate chips up into a triangle. "Yes," she had to admit. "I'd feel left out if she didn't tell me."

Desi nodded. "Exactly."

"I'll think about it," Juliet promised.

"Before we start the cookies," Desi said, wiping her hands, "I worried about this all night last night—come here and let me show you how to operate a pistol. You probably will never need to know, but there are some times you might need to have a gun, and I'd feel better knowing that I'd showed you."

"I don't want to shoot a gun, Desi!"

Desi rolled her eyes. "Don't be a baby. Just let me show you." She opened the gun cabinet and went through the steps of loading and firing both the rifle and the handgun. Juliet went along with it, but she couldn't imagine ever really using either one of them.

"Guns kind of give me the creeps," Juliet said.

"That's because you're in the city and people use them to kill other people. In the mountains, they make up for not having large, savage teeth and long claws."

Even Juliet had to chuckle at that. "I'll just hope I never have to use them then."

"I'm sure you never will." She went back to the

kitchen and popped a handful of chocolate chips in her mouth. "I'm so tired I could sleep for a year!"

The dogs exploded into a frenzy of barking, all of them racing to the front window that looked out toward the driveway. "Who's that, I wonder?" Desi said, wiping her hands on her apron.

Juliet was the first to see the flashing red lights. "Uh-oh."

She rose and went to the window, where she saw two vehicles with official Mariposa county shields on the sides. Lights on. "This looks official," she said, and turned around, lifting a hand, palm out, to caution Desi. "Don't say a single word, Desdemona, do you understand me? Not a word."

"You don't think they're arresting me, do you?" She widened her eyes. "I'm a vet! A *doctor.* We don't kill things, we save them. They can't really think I'd kill him?"

Juliet opened the door to the sheriff and two deputies, each dressed in green and khaki uniforms. "We're here for Desdemona Rousseau," one of the officers said.

Chapter 10

"She's here. You know her, right there."

"Desdemona Rousseau," the sheriff said, "You're under arrest for the murder of Claude Tsosie."

Looking stunned and shaky, Desi said, "I can't leave my sister. She doesn't know how to live up here in the mountains. By herself."

"Then she'd better get to town."

"Somebody has to look out for the property," Desi said. "The wolves—"

Juliet raised her palm. "Stop talking, Desi. I'll call Josh. You just go with them, we'll get you out in no time."

The sheriff snorted unpleasantly. "Not this time. Not in this town."

With hands that trembled visibly, Desi untied her

apron and came around the counter. She reached for her coat, hanging by the door. The sheriff pulled out a pair of handcuffs. Her face was the color of the flour on the counter.

Juliet protested. "Are handcuffs really necessary? She's obviously cooperating."

"Regulation," he said, but Juliet doubted it. He just wanted, for whatever reason, to make this more humiliating for her sister.

Once she had her coat on, Desi held out her wrists. The sheriff gruffly ordered her, "Turn around."

Desi's nostrils flared, a sign when they were children that you should clear the area. She turned around woodenly, and met Juliet's eyes as the handcuffs were fastened. "Don't stay alone," Desi said. "Call Josh, right now."

"I will," Juliet said. "Don't *worry.*"

Handcuffed, head down, Desi was led to the SUV. Over her shoulder she said, "*Now,* Juliet."

But Juliet waited until the SUVs had gone down the road into the pinkening dusk, her heart pounding so hard it felt her ribs would break. The case was circumstantial, it was true, but it was a very good circumstantial case. If they didn't find out who had really killed Claude, there was a very good chance Desi would at least go to trial. In a town so severely divided, that seemed like a very bad idea.

Whistling for the dogs, she headed back inside with the pack. She wondered if she ought to just go ahead and drive into town and find Josh rather than call him. But then she'd have to drive back up the narrow, twisting road in the dark. And, judging by the sky, the snow.

Josh's cell phone number was on the list taped to the wall and she dialed it with purposeful stabs. There was no answer until a voice mail message said, "This is Joshua Mad Calf. Leave a message."

Odd that he didn't answer the cell, especially as a cop. She frowned and said quickly, "Josh, this is Juliet Rousseau, and they just arrested my sister. I need your help."

She hung up and held the phone in her hand for a long moment, trying to decide what the best course of action would be. They'd have to set bail fairly quickly, but maybe not until Monday morning, which would mean Desi would molder in jail all weekend.

Beyond the uncurtained window, snow suddenly started to float down.

Great. Just great. She'd never learned to drive in the snow. And she *would* have just broken up with her boyfriend, who knew all sorts of things about criminal law that were unknown to her. She made a face. Who else could she call? Most of her friends were in entertainment or civil law.

No blinking neon sign came on in her imagination. No dancing choir came kicking through the room with placards around their necks. Outside, it was quickly getting dark, and the snow would begin to pile up, and her sister was going to jail for a crime she didn't commit.

Juliet hoped she hadn't committed, anyway. She was 99.9% sure, but her study of the law had shown her people did some pretty crazy things sometimes. Even people devoted to healing. Scorned lovers, in particular.

Her stomach plummeted. If she, Desi's sister, could think such things about a woman she'd known and loved all of her life, what would a jury think?

The phone in her hand rang suddenly and Juliet answered it breathlessly. "Hello?"

"Looks like your sister is finally going to get what she deserved," said a woman's voice.

For a moment, Juliet was stunned into silence. The line held a faint buzz, eerie and somehow menacing. "Who is this?"

But of course the threatening party didn't answer. Just hung up. Juliet pressed *69 to see if she could get a number, but the robotic voice simply said, "That number is unavailable."

Outside, the gloaming edged the peaks and the tops of the trees with an opal stain. Juliet wished she could enjoy it, but she walked over to a lamp and turned it on, her throat getting tighter and tighter. The idea of driving into town, without any clue of who she would seek out or what she'd do when she got there, seemed intimidating. Even worse was the idea of driving back here after she'd done whatever she'd done in town. Driving through the snow. On dark mountain roads in a little rental car not particularly designed for the task? No, thanks.

But even worse than that was the idea of staying here in the cabin alone. The uncurtained windows showing the whole world she was here by herself. The distance to town if anyone or anything—

What? She said to herself. Attacked? This wasn't a horror movie, with a deranged serial killer lurching through the high mountain forests of the San Juan range, or a rabid bear so hungry for blood he'd smash through windows and back doors.

And even in the event of murderers or wild animals, there were three dogs, wolf mixes that were enormously loyal to protect her. Three *big* dogs.

Still, she stood with the phone in her hand, her throat so tight she could barely breath, her heart pounding wildly. Tears stung the backs of her eyes and furiously, she blinked against them.

She was so tired of being afraid! Tired of being frozen. Tired of giving her whole life up to the possibility that something bad would happen again. Inside her head was a voice screaming: *just do something!*

And yet her body could not break free of its prison.

As Josh drove back to town from a call to a domestic dispute in the wilds beyond Mariposa Falls, he listened to Bonnie Raitt. He loved her better than any singer alive, loved her smoky voice and the richness of her sorrow. In her expressions of lusty love, lost and found, he connected with the sense of the mystical, as deep as any worship service. It was a passion he'd shared with Claude, actually. They'd spent many an enjoyable hour drinking ginger ale and listening to Bonnie. It was hard not to like Claude when he'd turned on the charm, and Josh, though he held himself aloof, had wanted to like the man.

What an absolute waste of a human being, he thought now. Claude had been born with talent, intelligence, charm and a very pretty face. He could have done anything, gone anywhere, and he'd actually started out on that path—earning a scholarship to college, working his way through, going into the Peace Corps after graduation. All the right things.

And yet, somewhere, he'd let himself get twisted into a parody, a Coyote thinking he knew more than he did.

Now he was dead.

Josh had taken himself off the case. He was too close to Desi, and the signs were pointing too hard toward her. He'd never be able to be objective about the evidence if it ended up pointing to her. Worse, he was afraid he'd ignore things he ought to notice.

Sometimes it wasn't possible to be both a good cop and a good friend. Josh had chosen friendship.

As the truck descended through an aspen grove in full blaze, the phone on his hip suddenly trilled with the message signal. A phone call had come in while he'd been out of range.

He punched the button to reach voice mail and held the phone to his ear. There were six new messages. *Six?* Good God.

The first two were from his mother, who told him that Glory had chipped a front tooth and had a dentist appointment on Monday morning—did he want Helene to take her? The second one was that Glory had asked permission to spend the night with one of her nursery school playmates and Helene was pretty sure Josh wouldn't want her to, but she'd promised Glory she would ask.

The third was a hang-up. The fourth was his boss with a very gruff order to call him immediately. There had been some news on the Tsosie case. The fifth was his boss again, repeating the message.

The sixth was Juliet, her voice wobbly as she reported the news that Desi had been arrested. He swore and pulled over to make phone calls properly.

Damn! He'd only been in the mountains for an hour and a half. How could so much have happened in such a short time? This morning, the skier Claude had been involved with had come in to make a report, and Josh had been concerned about her swollen eyes and shaky hands. She was pretty young, and it had to be traumatic to have a boyfriend murdered. Her alibi was airtight—she'd been drinking at The Black Crown with a group of Germans who were hiking the Mariposa trail. By the number of witnesses that had come forward, half the town must have been in the pub that night.

First, despite the urgency of everything else, he called his mother. "Is Glory all right? How did she chip her tooth?"

"She went down the slide facefirst before anyone could stop her." There was a mix of exasperation and pride and weariness in Helene's voice. "She has a mind of her own, that girl. It's not bad," she added, "and it's a tooth that'll come out in a year or two."

"Okay." Josh took a breath. "Mom, they arrested Desi a little while ago."

"Oh, no!"

"I'm going to the jail and see what I can find out, then go up and see her sister, and I'll be back after that."

"Why don't you just let Glory sleep here again? You go and get some real sleep. You sound beat."

He nodded. "All right. I'll let you know if I hear anything more."

"If you talk to Desi, give her my love."

"Will do."

When he hung up, he called Desi's home phone, and Juliet answered wearily. "I just got your message," he said. "Are you okay?"

"*I'm* fine. I'm worried about Desi, though. When will they have her arraignment? When can we get her out of there?"

"I'm going to town right now to see what I can find out." Snowflakes were floating out of the sky, sticking to his windshield and he frowned. "I want you to look around the cabin to make sure you have everything you'll need for three or four days, too. It could snow a lot with an Albuquerque low like this."

"You mean I could be stuck for three days up here by myself?"

"Easy." He turned the heater knob to defrost to melt the snow collected in little tufts over the windshield. "Look around and see what you might be missing. Water, food, firewood. We'll make sure you're prepared."

"You mean Desi might not get out of jail for *days?*"

He hesitated. The truth was, he doubted she'd be able to make bail at all if this shook out the way he thought it was going to. "Maybe, maybe not. Don't get all worked up about it just yet, though. Let me do some talking and see what I can find out."

He heard her take a breath and consciously release it. "Okay. Thanks."

"I'll be there in a little while."

He put the phone away and drove into town, worried on some low level at the way Juliet sounded. Not exactly frightened. Not panicky, which he could actually understand, given that she was a city girl and the mountains could be intimidating.

Something else. Hushed. As if a hand were pressing down on her. With a scowl, he resolved to get this taken care of as fast as possible, and then get up there and check on her.

And, he thought, maybe he should gently try to discover her story, whatever had traumatized her. It was obviously not resolved.

Juliet tried to pretend it was a normal night. She put some music on her MP3 player and stuck an earphone in her ear, determinedly singing along with the Black Eyed Peas and Dido as she creamed sugar and butter for the cookies Desi had started before she was arrested. The supplies were fine—she could survive for weeks on the food in the cupboards.

Outside, snow started to fall in a sturdy, determined way that seemed very different from the dinner-plate-sized flakes that had fallen her first night here. Once she'd read that the aboriginal peoples of Alaska had many names for snow, and this seemed a place where you'd want different names for it, too: Plate snow. Flurries. Blizzard snow. She stirred chocolate chips into the mix and stared out the window. This would be rain snow. Small flakes that were heavy enough to make a little bit of noise when they were falling steadily, as they were now. It was collecting more slowly than the other snow had, but with greater determination.

What if she was stuck here for three days, all alone?

Don't think about it.

Dropping spoonfuls of dough onto the cookie sheet, she tried to remember what it had been like to be brave, long ago. What had made her brave? She'd gone to college far away from her family, lived alone in an apartment in Berkley when she'd gone to law school, found her condo in Hollywood and lived there alone, in a neighborhood that was both good and bad, for several years. She'd traveled all over the U.S. by herself, stayed in hotels, navigated strange cities without much distress.

How had she done it?

The sound of a truck engine came to her as she took the last batch of cookies out of the oven. Juliet saw Josh, snow catching in his long glossy hair, headed across the yard.

He looked grim. Furious.

Beautiful.

His beauty struck her across the solar plexus, blazed into her throat. Against the snowy forest, with the very last of the daylight hanging in the clouds, he looked like an enchanted and ancient being emerging from the trees to visit the mortal realm for a moment. She wanted to put her hands in his hair, touch his cheekbones, kiss his throat, breathe in the enchantment.

She pressed her hand to the hollow of her throat, tried to brush the startling recognition off her face with her palm, and opened the door. "Did you see my sister?"

He shook his head, his mouth tight. "They wouldn't let me."

Gesturing him inside, she asked, "What did you find out? When will they set bail?"

"Very earliest is Wednesday. The judge is out of town until then."

Juliet narrowed her eyes. "Was that deliberate? The deputy who arrested her seemed to want it to be a very humiliating experience."

"Probably." He met her eyes. "It's a closed community in some ways. Desi has been accepted more than some because she is a great vet, but Claude made some enemies." He sounded calm, but his anger made his back too straight, his face stiff.

She offered a plate of cookies and Josh helped himself to a handful. "Wednesday! I hate thinking of her in there for so long."

"Me, too." He took a bite, then said, "I don't think you should stay here. It's pretty isolated and you're not used to it."

Relief moved through her like a wave of wind, cooling her fear. "I don't want to. But where will I go? I have to take care of the dogs, of the property, of—"

"You can come to my house. I have a big couch."

A ripple moved on her skin. She thought of kissing him earlier, thought of the flare that had burst over her nerves at the taste of his lips, the thrust of his tongue. To her embarrassment, her nipples pearled and she crossed her arms, hoping he hadn't noticed. She hesitated, picking up a cookie, then putting it down.

"I'm not expecting you to sleep with me," he said. "It's not like that."

Juliet blushed. "I didn't think you were."

"I just don't think you need to be up here by yourself."

"What about the dogs?"

"We'll bring them with us. Alex, the kid Desi loves so much, will take care of the wolf sanctuary. He's very capable."

Juliet really didn't have to weigh it out. Stay up here, terrified, or go to town with Josh? "I'll be right back," she said, going to pack a bag.

Chapter 11

Snow was really beginning to fall by the time they got to town. Juliet stood outside in it for a moment, the dogs leaping and dancing all around her as they heard Josh's dog, Jack, howling inside. In spite of everything, Juliet could not resist the delight of turning in a circle, looking around and up at the sky. It was enchantingly beautiful. "Snow is so magical," she said.

He chuckled. "See if you feel the same way in April."

There it was again, the assumption that she'd be hanging around. "I'm sure it loses some of its appeal."

"Let's get inside. I'll make us some supper. Unless you already ate?"

"I'm pretty sure fourteen chocolate chip cookies don't count for dinner."

The dogs tore inside and greeted Jack, and then Josh put them out in the backyard, which was fenced, to let them burn off some energy. "We'll have to take them out for a walk in the morning. Walk over and pick up Glory from my mom's house."

"Walk?"

He grinned, shrugged a little as he pushed his sleeves up on dark, smooth forearms. "Snowshoe, maybe. Have you ever tried it?"

"Nope."

"I need to give my mom a quick call," he said. "Go on into the kitchen if you want."

She followed him into the kitchen, a small room dominated by glass-fronted cabinets and a butcher block island in the center. Stools sat on one side, and the stove was in the middle of the island. The colors, peach and magenta and white, were a little weird, but in general, she liked it. In the hallway, Josh talked to his mother, explaining what had happened to Desi. He asked if Glory was still awake.

Then, "What?" he said. "I can't believe you let her go, Mom. That wasn't your decision to make."

Silence, the faint sound of a voice on the other end. "All right. I guess you're right." He paused. "Thanks, Ma. I don't know what I'd do without you."

Juliet pulled the sleeves of her sweater down over her hands, an old habit from childhood, and wondered with a pang what it would be like to have the kind of relationship with her mother that Josh obviously had with his. Her mouth curled at the corners in a bitter smile. Carol, the brilliant physicist with her tweeds, and blue blood, and trim waist, had better things to do than roll around in the emotional quagmire of children's needs.

Josh came into the kitchen. Juliet turned. "Everything okay?"

"I was hoping to go get Glory and bring her home before the snow, but my mom let her spend the night with a friend on the rez."

"And that's a problem?"

He lifted one shoulder, quickly, as if he knew his feelings were unreasonable. "I don't like her to be with anyone else but me or my mom. I only started letting Desi keep her a little while ago."

"Because of everything that happened with her mom?"

A terse nod. "It's all right. My mom has a point, too, that Glory needs to get to normal life. Part of that is spending the night with friends. My mom knows the family and trusts them." He blew out a breath. "It's hard for me to trust anybody these days."

"Yeah." Juliet found her mouth twisting again. "Yeah. I know what you mean."

"I noticed that." He reached for a pan on the stove. "Can you talk about it?"

"Not right this minute, if you don't mind." Like a curious dog, she rounded the perimeter of the kitchen, worrying her sleeves. "Is the color scheme your doing?"

"Hardly." He snorted. "Real estate is stupidly expensive around here, but there are some rentals set aside for the workforce. Most of them are down the valley quite a ways, but this whole section of blocks is rentals owned by the town. We have a place on the rez, of course, but it's a long way out, pretty isolated, and I need to be in town for Glory's sake." He pointed with a knife he'd taken out of the drawer. "My mom lives a couple of blocks over. She's the librarian."

"That's very convenient."

"No kidding. We worked at it." He sliced ham from a butt he'd taken out of the fridge, and dropped chunks of butter into a heavy cast-iron skillet. When the butter started to foam, he dropped the ham into it and sprinkled it lightly with brown sugar.

"That looks great," Juliet commented. "Can I do anything?"

"There's some canned pineapple in that cupboard to the left of the sink, if you want to get it out and open it. Can opener in the drawer below it. No, one more over."

He turned the heat down and let the butter and sugar caramelize with the ham. When Juliet opened the pineapple, he forked rings out and laid them on top of the ham slices, sprinkled them with a little more brown sugar and dots of butter, then turned the heat very low. "I'll let it just get good and hot. Do you like corn? Carrots?"

"Both." She leaned on her elbow. "I have to admit I was expecting something like a sandwich or something, not this actual supper."

He grinned. "Once upon a time, that's what it would have been. I had to learn to cook easy, healthy things so I could feed Glory."

"Lucky for me." She watched as he took frozen corn from the freezer and poured some into a bowl he put in the microwave, then filled a plump white teakettle with water and set it on another burner.

"Tea or milk or hot chocolate to drink?" he asked,

and opened a cupboard to reveal neat colorful boxes of tea in stacks.

"Oh, tea, definitely," she said, and chose a spice blend.

When they were settled over the very satisfying meal, Juliet said, "So, what will we do about Desi? Who else could have killed Claude?"

"Let's start with the people we know didn't do it," he said, buttering a chunk of hearty dark bread. "It wasn't Christie Lundgren, the girlfriend. She's got a rock-solid alibi. It wasn't you. It wasn't me."

Juliet raised her eyebrows. "That leaves a few possibilities."

"Right. I've done some poking around, and the trouble is—" He paused.

"The trouble is?"

"Claude made a lot of enemies the past couple of years." One thick brow cocked. "Mostly women and a few disgruntled boyfriends."

"I see." Juliet cut a triangle of ham, carefully layered a triangle of pineapple on top of it. "Criminal law isn't my specialty, but usually a crime of passion kind of murder seems to happen in the heat of the moment, or at least in the heat of the affair."

"That's true."

She ate the bite of ham, perfectly balanced salt and sweet, caramelized sugar, rich butter, crisp pineapple. "This," she said with deep appreciation, "is very good, Josh."

"Like it, little girl?" He winked. "I have many special dishes up my sleeve."

"Really." The word was droll. "As exciting as the

Vienna sausages and saltine crackers we had the other night?"

He laughed. "Point taken."

"So, anyway," she continued. "Who are the most recent scorned lovers?"

"That will take some digging, but it seems to be the dentist's wife. Who, in my opinion, would have been more likely to shoot Christie."

A little pause fell. "What about the developers who want the land? What if they've gone out of their way to frame Desi or something?"

Josh nodded, considering. "It's possible. There's a lot of money at stake, but we'll have to look into that some more. Might not be a bad idea to amble over to the Black Crown and see what the gossip around town has been."

"Is it open tonight?"

He raised his head. "Sure. You want to go?"

"What else is there to do, really?"

The corner of his mouth lifted, very, very slightly. "Nothing at all."

The Black Crown occupied a pub that had been serving libations to Mariposans as far back as the gold rush, though it had been called Molly's Tavern for most of that time. An ex-pro rugby player from New Zealand had purchased it two years ago and renovated it into a classic British-style pub that specialized in beers from around the world and old-fashioned pub food like hamburgers and shepherd's pie and even a ploughman's platter with cheeses and pickles that Glory loved.

Josh wasn't much of a drinker, but he liked Tamati Neville and his pub. Rugby jerseys lined the walls, and the jukebox had a great selection, and Tam kept order with a jovial smile backed up by muscle when necessary.

It was fairly busy tonight, especially for a night in the between times—between the summer tourists and hikers, before the winter ski crowds—and Josh glanced around, wondering why. A big group of skinny, tough runner types lounged in one corner, empty plates scattered on the table before them. One had an orange-and-white flag on his T-shirt: orienteering. Another group, mostly women, were dressed in athletic clothes, their leathery skin, sturdy thighs, and no-bullshit air giving away their adventure racer status.

Tam was behind the bar as always, a tall, athletic man with thick curly hair and bright, wolflike green eyes. "Hello, my friend Joshua," he said in his clipped Kiwi accent. "What can I get for you two?"

"Gossip is what I'm here for," Josh said, "but I'll have a bottle of whatever is on special tonight."

"And you, miss?" Tam asked. "We have beer from everywhere, but other things, too. What would you like?"

"What do you like best?"

"Well, I must admit to a soft spot for my native Tui."

"Okay. I'll have that." Juliet settled on the bar stool and glanced up at Josh, at which point he realized he'd been staring at her. The low light of the pub washed her blond hair with shimmery gloss, and he wanted to stroke the length of it, bury his hands in the softness. "What?" she asked.

He shook his head slowly, and lifted one hand to her hair, touching it very lightly with his palm. "Your hair is beautiful."

A flicker moved on her face. "Thanks."

Tam came back with their beers, and Josh raised his to toast Juliet. "Cheers," he said. She tapped his bottle with her own and they both drank.

"This is Juliet Rousseau," Josh said. "Her sister is the vet in town, and she runs the wolf center."

Tam said, "The one who was arrested today."

"Yep."

"I am sorry," Tam said, his accent slightly formal. "How can I help?"

"Claude drank in here, didn't he?"

Tam rolled his eyes. "Yeah. There was a bloody bastard, if there ever was one." He glanced at Juliet. "Sorry."

She smiled. "No problem. I agree with you."

Josh felt a sudden wish to puff out his chest and strut, or fling his arm out and claim her. Irritated with himself, he said, "So, did he bring his women in here?"

"Sure. Different bird every week."

"Anyone recently?"

"The skier. Before that, nobody in particular. All summer, he was feeding on the hikers with the tours."

Josh nodded. A local tour group brought hikers from all over the world to walk the Mariposa Falls Trail, part of a 238-mile loop that wandered through the Sangre de Cristos and the San Juan mountains. "Have you heard anything else?"

Tam leaned on the bar and his arms rippled. "I'll

keep my ears to the ground, mate, but not at the moment."

"Right. Thanks."

"Tam!" a tall, lovely blond woman cried from the other end of the bar. "A refill, love."

The big man grinned. "Duty calls." He started to head down the bar, then turned around. In a low voice, he said, "There was a woman with him a bit, off and on all summer. I dunno who she was, but she had money."

Josh took a notebook from his pocket. "Description?"

"Dark hair, green eyes. An accent from Europe. Maybe Germany or Poland or one of those, you know. That kind of accent."

"All right." Josh scribbled notes. "Age?"

He lifted a shoulder. "Maybe early thirties." With a swipe at the bar, he leaned in toward Juliet. "Ye ain't with this guy, are you?"

"Hey, man," Josh began.

But Juliet grinned. "Well, he's not as gorgeous as you are, but he's got great eyes."

"I reckon." He spotted the bar. "Come back under better circumstances."

Juliet shot a look up toward Josh, her eyes as blue as turquoises. A fine glitter danced there, a tease and a challenge. He let his gaze drop to her mouth and thought again of her kissing him, of the cool feel of her fingertips against his cheek, the plushness of her breasts against his chest.

"You're gonna have to quit looking at me like that," Josh said, and even he could hear the rumbling sound of his voice.

"Will I?" she asked, and put her small hand over the back of his big one. Beneath the bar, their thighs bumped. "Why?"

In other circumstances, he would have leaned over and accepted the invitation of that mouth. He would have thrust his tongue between her lips and laced his tongue with hers and inquired, in the most physical way possible, if she wanted to invite him in elsewhere. He was aching to touch her, undress her and look at her breasts and taste her pearling nipples. She had beautiful hair and beautiful eyes and a luscious mouth, and he wanted with a burning sort of energy, to explore her skin, see if it was as smooth as it looked. He loved blond hair. He loved pretty lips. He loved natural breasts, the squishy feel of them, the juicy jiggle. He imagined her nipples would be as pink as her tongue. Or perhaps dark and—

"You're looking at my breasts," Juliet said. "In American culture, that's considered rude."

"It's not rude in other cultures?"

She shook her head. "Not at all."

"Can we pretend we're in those other places?" He grinned. "I like looking at your breasts."

Juliet shifted, leaning back a little. "Better?"

He inhaled slowly, trying to calm his arousal. Leaning forward, he put his lips close to her ear and said quietly, "I could spend a whole evening on just your breasts."

"Could you?" she said, just as quietly. "Doing what?"

He raised his head and looked her in the eye. "It would be a lot more fun to just show you."

Juliet stood. "Okay."

Josh threw a ten-dollar bill on the bar and raised a hand at Tam. "Let's go."

She laughed softly and put her jacket on, tossing the long locks out of her collar and down her back, and headed for the door.

He knew the exact instant her flashback seized her. Her shoulders went rigid and she had a faint vacantness to her face. With an unnerving speed, she bolted through the door.

Damn. Josh bolted after her, catching up just as she skidded in the snow outside and fell flat on her belly, hitting hard enough he heard bones jar.

"Juliet!" He knelt at her side, tried to help her up.

But she fought him, her arms flailing, a dark noise coming from her throat. She gasped for breath, and he realized the wind had been knocked out of her. He blew in her face, as he did when Glory was a baby and cried so hard she lost her breath.

It didn't help immediately, and it was hard to hold on to her. The sidewalk was slippery with the slowly piling snow, and he skidded twice, feeling as if he was holding on to a fish that didn't want to be caught, or a wild horse. She bucked and flipped and twisted, fighting as if for her life. Blood came from her nose, and her hands were skinned raw, and she didn't seem to even notice.

Finally he grabbed a handful of snow and aimed for her face. She dodged and the bulk of it landed against her neck and chest, and for whatever reason, it did the trick. With a gasp, she caught her breath and her eyes focused on the moment. This moment.

"Hey," he said, sinking down against the wall. The street was deserted, the air filled with tiny steady pellets of snow. She was draped across his lap, blinking.

"Hey," she said, and swallowed. The tension in her body eased. "Sorry. I did it again."

"Can you walk?"

"Yeah. It's all mental, not physical." She stood up, brushed herself off, felt the blood on her face and looked at her glove. "Is it bad?"

Blood smeared from her nose and a cut above her eyebrow. He took snow from the window ledge and offered it to her. "We're only a few blocks away. Let's go get you cleaned up."

"Okay," she said. It seemed impossible it was the same word she'd uttered in such a saucy tone a few minutes before.

With as much gentleness as he could offer, Josh reached out and took her hand. She didn't pull away.

Juliet felt the stinging in her hands more acutely than anything. The palms were skinned raw, in a way she hadn't done since she was a child and had fallen on roller skates.

Depression crept in as they walked back, a sense of things going wrong, to never be put right again. Her sister rotting in jail, her own mind claimed by some wretched moment in the past. She felt doomed and defeated.

When they got to the house, the dogs rushed forward, sniffing her hands curiously. Josh's dog licked the stinging palms helpfully, and when the other dogs slumped by the fire, Jack padded behind the humans when they went to the bathroom.

It was a wonderfully old-fashioned room, with glass brick and tiny, art-deco era tiles on the walls. Jack trailed in after them, sniffed a corner, then the edge of her shoe, and settled in the hallway just outside the door as if keeping watch.

Juliet avoided looking at herself in the mirror, and turned on the water in the sink. "I can do it," she said.

"I know you *can,*" Josh replied. "Why don't you let me help you? I'd really like to."

Embarrassed, she lowered her eyes and plopped down on the toilet. "Okay."

A smile edged his voice. "You say okay a lot." He dipped a wash cloth in warm water. "Lift your chin."

She did, but still managed not to look at his face, instead focusing on the buttons traveling up his shirt. Off-white buttons in a green corduroy shirt. "So is the pub guy a friend of yours?"

"Acquaintance, I'd say. He was with a crew of smoke jumpers who were fighting the Hayman fire a few years back. You remember the Hayman fire?"

"No."

"It was a bad forest fire, the worst we've had in Colorado in decades. They were fighting it for weeks, and it took a lot of manpower." Gently, he wiped blood from her face. "Tam and another guy had a bad landing—he broke his leg and his friend died. Don't move."

He ran cold water over the cloth and pressed it to her eyebrow. "This one is bleeding pretty good. You might need a stitch."

She didn't say anything, remembering another night,

another time her face was gently wiped clean of blood. Her throat felt tight.

"It might be a good idea to talk about this," Josh said. "Maybe tell me what happened?"

A half hour ago, she'd been thinking only about how it would feel to have Josh's arms around her, taste his mouth, feel his hands. She'd been thinking about what his body would look like without clothes and how it might feel to have the attention he promised—*an evening on your breasts*—and then, some wretched something had yanked her back in time again, and it had been bad, this time, a sense of panic so acute and overwhelming that she'd barely been able to breathe.

"I feel so cheated," she said dully.

He sank down on the bathtub, putting their faces on the same level, and brushed hair away from her forehead. "Cheated how?"

His eyes were that soft deer-brown, the lashes so very long and childlike, softening the hard lines of cheekbone and jaw. His hands, brushing that hair away, were gentle as feathers. "I haven't been able to feel much of anything for a long time, and there I was, wanting you in a real way, wanting to kiss you and—" She lifted a shoulder. "And then something in my brain or memory kicks in and it's like I've made no progress at all."

"Were you raped?"

She bowed her head, ashamed. It was so humiliating, every time, to have to admit it. "A little more than a year ago." With exasperation, she said, "I don't know why I can't seem to get over it, process it, be done with it. I mean, he barely even hurt me. As these things go, it wasn't that bad."

"Oh, Juliet," he said, taking her hand and carrying her knuckles to his lips. "That's like saying you were only murdered with a single gunshot instead of knifed. It's horrible."

She shrugged. "Maybe."

He pressed the cloth to her eyebrow again. "Have you had any counseling for PTSD? They have some better techniques these days."

"I've had counseling. I really think I'm doing okay. It's just that a couple of times lately, I've had some bad moments."

"Right. I can see that you're pretty functional. Smart. All that stuff." He smiled. "But you're also having some pretty serious flashbacks and that's going to make life tough to manage."

"Have you had some training in PTSD or something?"

He raised his eyebrows. "I studied it on my own. In case Glory had symptoms, I'd know what to do."

"I see."

"Tell you what," he said. "Let's go make some hot chocolate and look through the video collection and see what looks good. What do you say?"

"I'm not an invalid," Juliet said with some irritation. "I don't need special treatment."

"Okay, Hop-A-Long."

She scowled at him. "What does that mean?"

He stood and held out a hand. "Come on. Let's go make something good and watch television and let the rest of the world go by for a couple of hours. How does that sound?"

For a moment, she hesitated, then put her hand in his and let herself be hauled to her feet. "Pretty damned good."

The dogs, excited, ran for the back door, looking over their backs to make sure the humans were getting the message. Juliet let herself laugh, let the day shake free from her shoulders. "Think they might want to get out?"

They all traipsed down the hall, into the kitchen, and Josh opened the back door. He whistled. "Well, it's coming down now. Look at that."

She peeked out over his shoulder. "Dinner plate snow!" she cried. "It's so pretty."

"It is. Now don't you think hot chocolate seems like the right idea?"

"Yeah," she said. "It does."

As she stood there, she thought of her sister, out in the darkness last night. "I am so worried about Desi," she said quietly.

"So am I," he said.

"We have to find out who did this," Juliet said. "I keep worrying that it looks bad for her. That if *I* can think the worst—"

"The worst?"

Juliet raised her eyes. "That she killed him." There, she'd said it.

He took a breath. "We have to find out the truth."

"Are you afraid of what you might find?"

"Maybe a little," he said, and brushed a lock of hair off her cheek, tucked it behind her ear. "But it's always better to know the real truth of a thing."

"Is it?" she asked. A fierceness rose in her. "I'd lie to protect her, Josh."

His smile quirked sideways. "So would I. So would my mother and her cronies. So would a lot of people. Let's cross that bridge when we come to it, huh?" He took her hand. "Come on, let's get some refreshments."

Chapter 12

Josh built a fire and made a tray with cookies, cups, a fat pot for the hot chocolate, even some marshmallows. While he was getting it ready, Juliet dutifully flipped through his extensive DVD collection. It contained a fair number of race-car and football movies, along with what appeared to be every James Bond ever made, and all the original *Mission: Impossible* television series. There were Disney cartoons she assumed belonged to Glory.

But Juliet was also delighted to discover her favorite kind of movie: big dramas, not the usual black-and-white comedies so many people seemed to collect these days, but war movies and tragedies. She saw *The English Patient* and *Dangerous Liaisons* and— "*Dr. Zhivago!* You have actually seen this movie?"

"Oh, yeah. My mother loves it. I've watched it with her a million times." Kneeling by the fire, Josh grinned over his shoulder. "Julie Christie is hot."

Juliet grinned. "She's blond, right?"

The lights flickered suddenly. Went out. "Uh-oh," Josh said. "I forgot to mention the power is a little wonky during heavy snows. The lines are still all overhead in this part of town."

Juliet leaned back on her heels. As always, the quiet left behind by a power outage always amazed her. The hush filled the rooms, and then the lights blinked back on. They wavered, then held.

"I'm going to get some candles," Josh said. "Go ahead and put the movie in if you want."

"Really? You'll watch *Dr. Zhivago?*"

"Sure, why not? We might lose power, but we might not."

"That's not what I meant." Juliet handed him the case. "I am *so* not going to argue with you. Pop that baby in before you change your mind."

He chuckled. "I won't change my mind." He headed into the kitchen, and came back with three fat candles on saucers.

Settling on the couch in her socks, Juliet plucked a marshmallow off the tray. "If I ever told my friends that a guy watched *Dr. Zhivago* with me there would be a line of women from your door around the block."

"Yeah?" He put the DVD in and came around the coffee table to sit next to her. "All this time, that was all I had to do? Tell women I loved sappy old movies?"

Juliet thought about it. "Yes. Pretty much."

"Damn. Somebody should have told me." He held the remote control in his hand, put his other hand on her leg. "Are you okay now?"

"Yes. Play the movie."

He did.

She knew it was just a distraction, a way to keep her mind off Desi, but Juliet loved *Dr. Zhivago.* Loved everything about it—the music, the costumes, the handsome, tortured face of Omar Sharif, the beautiful landscapes, the sad, sad story.

It was delicious to be curled up on the couch in front of a fire, watching it with Josh, too. They nibbled cookies and popcorn, drank hot chocolate. At one point, he put his arm around her, and Juliet did not object. She snuggled into his broad side and let the smell of him fill her, enjoyed the pleasure of his body next to her own, so warm and real. It was both comfortable and arousing to be so close.

It felt wonderful, and she tried to remember a time she simply watched a movie on video with a guy.

When the movie ended, so tragically and so poignantly, Juliet was wiping tears away surreptitiously when Josh handed her a tissue and stood up. "I'll be back with your pillows. Do you want anything to drink?"

Disappointed that he was headed off to bed so abruptly, Juliet shook her head. The lights flickered, and she suddenly wanted them to go out, for the room to be plunged into blackness only lit with the embers of the fire and candles. She wanted to kiss him, to explore his mouth and those broad shoulders and—

Well, whatever else.

And really, what was stopping her from taking the initiative?

Did she dare? She did. Standing up, she turned off the lamp, then lit the candles on the coffee table. The fire had gone low, and she padded over to it in her stocking feet to see if she could figure out how to feed some more wood to the flames.

"This is nice," Josh said, coming back into the room with pillows and blankets. He had to step around and over dogs, who groaned in pleased ways when he nudged them, and dumped the linens on a chair. "Does this mean you might not be ready to go right to sleep?"

Juliet smiled over her shoulder. "Maybe. I just kept wishing for the lights to go out and I decided maybe it would be okay if I just turned them off." She held a smallish log in her hands. "Is this the right size to feed it right now?"

"Perfect." He came around the coffee table and knelt next to her, picked up the poker and sent sparks sailing up the chimney. "Put another one on, too, in case we do lose power."

Juliet felt a low singing pleasure rising through her veins as she put the log on the fire. Flames began to lick the new wood and heated her skin on the front of her body, and she leaned back on her heels, putting her hands on her thighs. "Beautiful, isn't it?" Juliet said.

Kneeling next to her, Josh brushed hair away from her face. "Yes," he said, and leaned down to kiss her.

Juliet met his lips eagerly, and they kissed for a long time, just that. Lips weaving together, sliding, sipping.

Tongues dashing out, dipping in, lacing together. Just lips, his and hers, and the languorous rise of sap in her blood, delicious and almost forgotten. The rush of sensation over her spine, the softening of her thighs, the catch in her breath as she imagined his hands on her. She shifted, raising a hand to his jaw and he made a low, pleased noise, and tumbled her sideways to the floor. They laughed a little as they landed.

"If we're going to make out in front of the fire, maybe we ought to get a blanket," Juliet said, amazed at the throatiness of her tone.

"I just happen to have one right over here," he said, and leapt up, grabbing the thick down comforter from the chair and spreading it in front of the fire, then kneeling down and pulling Juliet onto it with him. He tossed a pillow down and Juliet nabbed it, smiling up at him.

For one minute, he looked demolished and overwhelmed. "Juliet, you are so beautiful."

"Am I?"

"Oh, yeah." He kissed her lips, lightly, and her chin. "Can I ask a question?"

"Sure."

"Do you have any issues with sex? I mean, not that we have to do anything but lie here and kiss, but if there are things I should know, maybe you should tell me?"

Juliet gazed up at him. "I don't have any that I know of. All I know is that I feel something when you touch me, and that's new."

His eyelids grew sleepy. "Yeah? What do you feel?"

"Kiss me again and let me see if I can tell you."

He made a soft noise and covered her mouth with his own, a hot tongue and hot lips lighting tiny explosions of peppermint fire over her brow, and a smoky surprise at the base of her throat, and an electric zing down her spine. "Oh," she whispered, "I feel like kissing you for about a hundred years."

"We can do that," Josh said, and kissed her again. "And if I kiss you here?" he said, pressing his lips to her throat. "How is that?"

"Oh, I don't know," she said, her breath coming a little higher in her throat. "You might have to do it again."

"I can do that," he said, and opened his mouth and dragged his tongue down the column of her throat, lingering in a circle over the hollow between her collarbones. Slowly, slowly, he made his way back up, his tongue making lazy circles on her flesh, his mouth pausing to take little sharp sucks. Juliet closed her eyes and luxuriated in the pleasure he gave, letting her hands move on his broad shoulders. The fire warmed her feet and lent a quiet counterpoint to the sound of their breath and the little exclamations of surprise and discovery.

He worked his way back to her mouth and plunged this time with barely concealed passion, his tongue thrusting, his body hard against hers, his hands on her shoulders.

Juliet ached to feel his chest, taste his skin, and she pushed away enough to put her hands on his shirt. "I need this off," she said. "I want to see."

He rose on his knees and stripped the shirt off, his eyes fixed on her face. Pale orange firelight spilled over his naked torso, illuminating his broad shoulders, his lean waist. She lifted a hand and traced the round of his navel, and the silky hair against her finger sent a shock wave through her body, straight between her legs. With a boldness that was unlike her, she sat up and kissed his belly there.

"Now you," he said.

Juliet knelt, too, and started to unbutton her blouse. "Let me do it," he said, and she dropped her hands. He reached up to unfasten the first buttons, then the next, the next, and spread the cloth open to show her belly, her bra. He did not move fast, seeming to relish every moment of revelation, and Juliet felt a wild wave of desire washing over her, wave after wave making her dizzy and hungry. "Touch me," she whispered.

His smile was very small. "All in good time." His hand glided beneath the fabric of her blouse, across her shoulders, then down her sides, skimming the shirt off of her. The bra was a back closure, and he reached around and undid that, too. Juliet arched her back and held her arms down so he could take it off, feeling her breasts spill into freedom, into firelight.

He tossed the scrap of fabric aside and put his hands on his thighs, simply looking at her toplessness, at her eyes, then her shoulders and neck, then her breasts. She gazed back at him, at the black crown of his head, the beauty of his well-formed shoulders, the sleek nakedness of skin just inches away, and thought she would faint dead away of desire. It buzzed through her mind, through her forehead, her groin, pearled in perfect, beaming lights at the tips of her breasts which wanted—

He bent and opened his mouth around her right

nipple and suckled lightly. Juliet cried out softly. He raised his head. "Is that okay?"

"Yes." The word was a breathy whisper.

He bent and did it again, opened his hot, wet mouth and settled it with no hurry and great skill on her nipple. He sucked lightly, and wound his tongue around it, and let go, and started again on the other side. At just the moment she felt she would fly away if he didn't somehow ground her, capture her, he raised his hands and cupped her flesh in his big palms and kissed them all over.

"Your breasts are beautiful, too," he said with a raw sound, "as beautiful as your hair and your eyes and your mouth." He gathered her up into his lap and kissed her lips, and Juliet cried out at the explosion of feelings that brought, flinging her arms around his shoulders, pressing them close together. He pulled her hips down and into his aroused member, thrusting slightly upward. His hands skimmed up and down her back, buried themselves in her hair, and Juliet felt as if she was a being of pure light, radiating heat and desire and relief.

His hair. Heavy and cool, like the skirt of a bridesmaid's dress she'd worn once. Juliet lifted her arms so she could feel it on her skin and kissed him, over and over.

A huge noise slammed into the placid moment, and both of them grabbed on to the other, looking to see what happened. The lights did go off.

"What was that?" Juliet cried.

Josh grabbed the quilt and tugged it around her shoulders, wrapping them up closely. "I don't know." He was still, listening, and Juliet listened, too, hearing only the fire and the wind outside. "I should go look around," he said.

She nodded, climbing reluctantly off his lap. He kissed her head and moved away in his bare feet. Juliet watched him go round the house, beautiful and strong and gigantic, a man she could fall in love with.

But with a rush of disorientation, she thought, *how did I get here?* With a man she hadn't even known existed a few weeks ago, taking off her clothes with him, getting ready to—as they used to say to each other—go all the way?

One of the dogs got up, Jack, and wandered over to sit with her, falling down beside her with a great, wuffling sigh. Juliet put a hand in his fur and stared at the leaping, crackling flames, feeling suddenly dizzy. She'd broken up with her fiancé. Her sister had been arrested. Claude, who had been her brother-in-law for more than ten years, was murdered.

"A tree fell over in the street," Josh said, coming back into the room.

Juliet looked up at him. Nodded.

He sat down beside her. "You okay?" He put a hand on her back, just one flat hand.

It was enough. As if someone flipped a switch, Juliet felt the panic rise up in her, the unreasoning need to flee, and she gripped the dog's fur more tightly than she intended. He yelped and gave her a wounded look, and Juliet, horrified, let go. Blindly, she reached for Josh. "Help!" she whispered.

He grabbed her hand and held on tightly. "It's all right, Juliet. I'm here. I'm right here."

And this time, it faded fast. She took a breath. "You must really think I'm wacko."

He put his arms around her, the blanket between them. "No. I wish I knew how to help."

Juliet didn't speak for a moment, letting herself rest against his broad chest, feeling the solid strength of his arms around her. She raised her arms and put her hands on his wrists, and they stared into the orange-and-yellow fire. "I feel safe with you," she said finally, and pressed her lips to his wrists. "But in general, I'm *so* afraid, all the time, and I'm so tired of it. It's exhausting."

"I know." He nestled his head close to hers, kissed her shoulder. "Do you want to tell me about what happened?"

Juliet paused. "People don't really want to hear about it, Josh. You think you do, but then the reality is boring and ugly and it changes the way you look at me."

"That might be true of some people," he said, "but I'm a cop, remember? It won't shock me and it won't make me think differently about you." He made his legs into a diamond that fit around her knees, so she was entirely protected with his body. "All that said, if you don't like or don't want to talk, it's okay. It just kinda seems like maybe you've got a boil that needs lancing."

"Maybe so," Juliet said. She took a breath and said, "I was on a business trip for my firm. I'd just had dinner at the hotel restaurant and I went outside."

In a steady, plain voice, she told him the story, factually and without elaboration or hysterics. As she got to the end, when she was finally home, two days later, and could not go to sleep in her own bed, she realized tears were streaming down her cheeks, and Josh was ever-so-gently rocking her, side to side.

She was half-naked beneath the blanket. Her sister was in jail. Claude was dead and she'd broken up with Scott, and nothing seemed the way it should…except Josh. There was something so unbelievably, perfectly right about his arms around her, his gentle rocking, the feeling of his nose in her hair as she wept. Wept and wept and wept, for all the darkness in the world and all the women who had ever been raped and her sister who had a broken heart and Claude, who was dead.

And all through it, Josh held her. A blessing.

When Juliet was finally spent, her tears leaking out of her in a long, slow stream, never noisy, never hysterical, but steady and seemingly endless, he helped her into a T-shirt from his closet and put her to bed in his own bed.

Exhausted, she said, "Thank you," and fell asleep so hard he thought she'd probably be there a long, long while.

He, too, was exhausted, and slipped between the covers next to her, cradling her curvy self into his belly. She shuddered in post-weeping release, and allowed herself to be cuddled, lifting his hand to her mouth before falling back over the cliff to her rest.

And then, he too, was asleep, carried away into a restless world of vivid, violent dreams where a cat was tearing apart a rapist, where Desi was sitting in a jail cell crying out his name, where the silence seemed vast and endless and terrifying. Over and over, he surfaced the slightest bit to discover the Juliet part of the dreams was real, that she was still in his bed, still sleeping soundly, protected and safe in his arms.

When he started awake suddenly to find that circle empty, it was light outside, and he heard Juliet in the bathroom, running water. She came back out, and when she found him awake and looking at her, she paused.

"You look so beautiful," he said, and it was true. Her hair, the shimmery color of the lemon crayon in Glory's box, was mussed and tumbling over her slim shoulders in the plain white T-shirt and a pair of underwear.

"Do I?" she said with a laugh and looked down. "I was coming back, if that's okay. I didn't mean to wake you."

Wordlessly, he flipped the covers back and made a place for her. As she crossed the room, her breasts, bare beneath the T-shirt, swayed and bobbled, a sight that made him instantly, furiously hard.

At the edge of the bed, she showed him a small foil packet. "I hope you don't mind," she said, "but I found this in the bathroom cabinet."

"I don't mind," he said. If there was any more blood in his organ, it would explode, but more surged in when she reached down, grabbed the bottom of her T-shirt and pulled it off over her head.

For one moment, she stood there, pink and white and blond, her skin smooth and pale, her tummy slightly rounded, her shoulders delicate like butterfly wings, and her breasts, white and round and full, tipped with pearly pink nipples.

He pulled the covers further back, showing his bare upper body and the raging hard-on in his briefs. Lightly he touched himself and said, "See what you're doing to me?"

One impish eyebrow lifted. "Very nice."

Josh said, "Come here."

She did, flowing forward to put her body against his, naked chest to naked chest, legs tangling, mouths open to absorb, inhale, meld. Hands tangled in hair, his and hers, hers and his. He tasted her lips, her chin, her neck. She straddled his erection and he groaned at the heat and pleasure of her rubbing against him. He held her hips and rose up, bending her slightly backward in his lap so he could take a nipple into his mouth and play with it, teasing with his tongue, sucking and letting go, using his fingers on her other one, until she was whimpering softly in longing, her hips moving restlessly against him, hot and damp and ready.

But not as ready as she would be. He slid his fingers between them, beneath her panties and into the layers of folds beneath, all trembling and shivery. His organ throbbed in furious desire as he rubbed her, slowly, deeply, bringing out a rhythm of cries, a bucking hunger. When he knew she was very, very close, he stopped.

Her blue eyes flew open. "Josh," she panted. "I've never…this is—"

He kissed her, thrusting his tongue deep into her mouth, and rolled them over until he was on top, it took a moment of fumbling to get rid of the fabric between them and another moment to sheath himself properly, but Juliet was like cake falling to pieces beneath him, and when he nudged her legs apart, reached down to ease himself into her, she cried out in guttural pleasure, that rich, panting sound of mindless, pure, physical enjoyment. His own flanks quivered at the pleasure of her around him, the beauty of that tousled hair on his pillow, her pink and white breasts straining upward for his mouth, her legs wrapping around him and pulling him home with surprising strength. She pulled him in with strong arms.

They kissed, and it was a rocket of sensation, touch, sound, movement, a pleasure so profound and rich and earthy Josh wanted to stay right there, an orgasm building in his loins by degrees. Go go go go, nerves, lips, legs, hands, tongues. Her hair tangling in his fingers. Her breasts, her belly, her sex pulsing like a squeezing fist around him as she came, crying out with a high, blistered keening. He tumbled right after her.

And then it was the next best thing, the first moments afterward. He kissed her and kissed her, her breasts all sweaty against his chest, their breath still coming fast, his organ doing that last little throb, uh uh uh, and she was pulsing around him now and then, the little aftershocks.

"Wow," Juliet said, blinking up at him.

He grinned down at her. "Have a pretty good time, did you?"

"Uh, yeah." She raised a hand and brushed hair over his shoulder. "You're amazing."

"It's you. Or us." He realized how heavy he must be and made a move to slide sideways. "Or something."

She sighed as he left her, making a sound of soft regret. "Come on back now, anytime," she said, and laughed, putting her head against his arm. It was a giggle, a sound of pure, unfettered pleasure.

"You sound pretty happy."

"Wonder why?" She put her finger on her cheek, looking exaggeratedly vacuous. "I've only just had great sex with the sexiest guy I've run into in years—"

"Only years? Is there someone better than me out there?"

"Okay, ever. And I slept like a baby, and it snowed a lot less than I thought it was going to."

"Really?" He flipped the covers off his body and jumped up to peek outside. The snow was spitting a little, but he could tell from long experience that it wouldn't be long until the sun burst through the clouds. Snow had definitely piled up in corners, but it was more the sort of accumulation that came of wind. "It should be gone by suppertime, I'm guessing. Maybe sooner."

She'd propped herself up on the pillow and inclined her head, frankly admiring him. "You, Mr. Mad Calf, have very, very nice legs."

He grinned, and turned around. "Yeah? Anything else you like?"

Her eyes looked suddenly smoky, and there was the faintest betraying flare of her nostrils. "Everything," she said distinctly.

It was cold. He dived back into the bed. And they did it all again.

After a long, luxurious, *hot* shower, Juliet found Josh in the kitchen, watching the news on a tiny white television set. The scent of bacon frying and coffee brewing perfumed the air, and there were agreeable piles of food lined up on the counter—eggs, cheese, apples.

But for a moment, Juliet was seized with a sense of

surprise, looking at Josh himself. At his long, powerful legs, his graceful hands, the thick black fall of his hair.

She'd taken a new lover! How amazing!

And what a lover—every cell in her body felt properly tended for the first time in a very long time, as if every inch of her had been taken out, washed, dried, brushed, and put back into place.

Her mind, her heart, all those places that ordinarily sent out objections and got so noisily involved in these things, were strangely silent. "What's your pleasure, my lady?" Josh asked, gesturing toward the supplies on the counter. "Omelets with cheese, bacon on the side?"

She grinned. "A girl could get used to this."

He wiggled his dark brows. "Promises, promises."

"What are you having?"

"Omelets, bacon on the side, coffee."

"I'll have that, too. Do you want some help?"

He gave her an ironic grin. "You just sit there and look purty, little lady." From the cupboard, he took a cup and poured coffee into it. "Milk's right there."

On the television, a newscaster showed the ski slopes in Aspen, and a shot of a beautiful blond woman. "Josh, look! It's Christie Lundgren. On the news. Turn it up!"

The newscaster said, "—Lundgren was said to be in a heated relationship with the artist who was murdered two days ago in the glitzy ski resort town of Mariposa."

Josh pointed to a banner below the picture. "It's an old picture of Christie," he said. The banner read photo January 2004.

"Prominent Aspen art dealer Renate Franz has issued a statement that her collection of Tsosie art will be on display through the end of the month, when she will hold an auction."

A photo of an elegant, tiny woman with a wealth of dark hair stepped in front of the camera, visibly upset. "We're all grieving," she said. "The world has lost a major talent and a man we will mourn for years to come."

Josh said, "German accent, you think? How old do you think she is?"

"Thirties?" At first, Juliet didn't make the connection. Then she turned back to the screen. "Ah! Do you think she might be the one Claude was with last summer? An art dealer?"

Josh frowned. "I think she had more than art on her mind."

On the television, the newscaster wrapped it up. "Investigations are continuing, but Tsosie's wife, Desdemona Rousseau, has been arrested."

Juliet's stomach flipped. She wondered if her sister Miranda had seen this story. "I've gotta call my other sister after breakfast."

"We need to go talk to Desi, too, make sure she's all right."

Spiraling tension rose through Juliet's chest, tightening and compressing her lungs. *Breathe,* she told herself. They would get to the bottom of this. She stood up, shaking off the anxiety, and peered out the window. There were still heavy clouds overhead, but the snow had stopped falling. The tiny pellets, the rain-snow, had not particularly piled up, though the wind had blown it into drifts here and there.

It was plenty for the dogs, however. They pranced

around in it happily, dancing, dodging, almost laughing aloud. "The dogs look very happy," she commented and watched them as they played with each other, bowing down, throwing up tufts of snow, getting covered with it. "I was never much of a dog person before Desi got so wrapped up with the wolves, but there's really nothing like them."

At the stove, Josh turned slightly to indicate he was listening. "What do you mean?"

She lifted a shoulder. "They're so...fluffy and happy and devoted." Faithful, she wanted to add, but didn't, afraid it would be too leading. In the yard Crazy Horse dashed away from a charge by Tecumseh and she could almost hear him laughing. "They make me feel protective and protected."

"I love dogs. When I was in the army, it was impossible to keep them and it was terrible. I missed having a dog every single day." He smiled. "I love it that I can leave for five minutes, come back, and there's Jack, at the door, dancing around like I've been gone for three days."

"I'll have to get a dog when I go back to Hollywood."

His head jerked up. "Are you going back?"

"I have a life there." Used to have a job. "A condo."

"Right. I get it."

Juliet looked at him. "You sound angry." She had considered not going back, but what did his reaction mean? Did she want to get so involved?

"Sorry." He focused on the eggs, very gently flipping them over their filling. "I'm not. I just have to remember not to let Glory get too attached."

Juliet crossed her arms and sat down. "Maybe you

should drive me back up the mountain before she comes home."

He brought the pan over to the island and slid the omelet out on to the plate. "Do you have any idea how much snow is up there right now? We'll go get her this afternoon, but you're not going up that mountain for at least a day."

Juliet looked at the steaming eggs and her stomach growled. He passed her a plate of bacon. "So what do you want to do?"

"Just don't give her any false promises," Josh said. "That's all."

The back of his neck looked stiff and she wondered if she'd been rash to sleep with him. "I didn't mean to lead you on, Josh. I thought we were grown-ups here…. I…" She looked at him, feeling both rejected and pleased at his jealousy and pierced at the possibility that—what? He wanted her here? "I'm sorry."

With a thud, he put the pan down and came around the island. With a sexy, vulnerable forcefulness, he took her face in his hands and kissed her. "No, I'm sorry," he said. "I'm being an ass. It's not your fault that Glory thinks you're a princess. It's not your fault her mother let her down. It's not your fault that I wish you lived here instead of in California."

She put her hands on his, holding him there, aware of a thudding something in her chest—some strong, unacknowledged emotion. "Josh, I'm pretty much a mess right now. I lost my job. I haven't been able to do anything much for a year. I don't know that I'm ever going to be any better, okay?" A wave of that volatility she'd felt last night struck the back of her eyes and she blinked hard. "Please don't make me cry again."

He kissed her. First her mouth, then her eyelids, one at a time. He raised his head and looked at her. "Can I tell you, Juliet, that you really are getting under my skin? I'm not used to it."

"Me, either."

"You are one of the prettiest women I've ever met."

She smiled. "You can tell me that anytime."

"And I love your mouth. And your breasts. And your eyes."

"All those things."

His dark eyes looked serious. "You also have a lot of heart. Like a lion." He touched her nose lightly. "And I've been known to be just a little bit...intense."

She captured his wrists before he could pull away. "You have given me more peace in twenty-four hours than I've had in many, many months, Josh. I just don't know myself well enough to know what any of it means today. Is that okay?"

"It's fine." He let her go and went back to his side of the island. "Let's eat, then I'll find out where Glory is and maybe we can go snowshoeing or for a walk, depending on how the paths look. What do you think?"

"Excellent," she said, and cut a generous piece of omelet. "Not, however, as perfect as this."

"Don't suppose you brought any hiking boots down with you."

Juliet tossed her hair over her shoulder. "No. But I have a credit card. I bet there are hiking boots for sale somewhere in this town."

"You'll pay with blisters if you do that."

She shrugged. "We don't have to hike to Timbuktu, do we? I mean, I like hiking, but it's been awhile, and maybe just a *little* hike would be fun."

He grinned. "That's a possibility." He, too, busied himself with the food. "I'm starving."

Juliet laughed, and the sound was as much like a giggle as she ever gave. "We did have quite a workout."

His eyes crinkled up. "So we did." He took a big gulp of milk. "Do you think you could curl her hair?"

"Glory's?" Juliet asked. "I don't know. What do you have around here?"

"Nothing I know of."

"We can always use rags. I know how to do rag curls. Or we can buy curlers in town."

He nodded. "The other thing we need to talk about is what to do about Desi's bail."

"Setting it? Or getting her out?"

"Paying it once it's set."

"The land is worth a fortune," Juliet said. "But I think she'll protest using it as a guarantee for bail."

"Might not have any choice."

Juliet thought about it for a few minutes. Thought of everything Desi had gone through to secure that land, hold on to it—and not for herself, but for her wolves. "No," she said. "If we have to, I'll use my condo. It's worth plenty."

Josh put his knife and fork neatly over his plate, tines down. "What about your parents? Sounds like they have a few resources."

"They do, but they don't particularly like to dip into

them. They'd be horrified over the scandal attached to this."

"Who are these people?" Josh asked in an irritable tone. "You and Desi both make them sound like monsters, but they raised both of you. You're not monsters, either one of you."

Juliet nodded. "I know. There's the paradox. I can't explain it, either." She touched her napkin to her lips. "My mother is an old-fashioned WASP, a blue blood back to who knows when. Trouble is, she had this amazing brain for physics and she thought she should pursue it, and instead of marrying some Massachusetts-blooded stallion, she met my father, a poet, who swept her off her feet."

"That's romantic."

Juliet shrugged. "I guess. They think it is." He looked so bewildered she shook her head. "They're great at being scientist and poet and grand lovers to each other. They were just rotten at being parents."

Josh crossed his arms, his beautiful mouth taut with skepticism. "Rotten how? Did you have to spend too much time with the nanny or something?"

"Are you being a snob, Mr. Mad Calf? If you have your physical needs covered, everything's all right? Is that it?"

"I made you mad, I'm sorry." He took a breath. "But to be honest, it is kind of a stretch to believe that you suffered much."

"Honestly, I didn't suffer as much as the other two. Not sure why. I was always such an innocent, you know, that maybe some of it just didn't get through." She met his eyes. "But for example, my mother does not know

I was raped, and she won't. She'd hate to know about it, and it would end up being my fault somehow, and I'm just not going to go through all that."

"You can borrow my mom if you want."

"I just might." With a sigh, she said, "If you ever meet them, you'll see what I mean."

"I believe you."

"No, you don't," she said. "But that's okay."

Chapter 13

The morning was pristine, and once they moved out of Josh's pocket neighborhood, there wasn't as much snow as it had first appeared. In town, business seemed a little slower than normal, but the ReNew café and the pancake house were open for business, shoveling snow off the sidewalk into the street, where a fast-moving stream of melting snow ran down the gutter.

"It's weird how fast the weather changes around here," Juliet said. "Blizzard to sunshine in five seconds flat." She kicked the slush on the sidewalk. "How long will it take to melt?"

"A day at these temperatures," he said. "But it won't be long until there's snow everywhere, all winter." He gestured to an outdoor wear store. "Let's get you some boots, huh? We'll hike up to the shrine. It should be fairly accessible."

"The shrine?"

"Our Lady of the Butterflies. She's famous. You don't know about her?"

Juliet nodded. "I know. We used to come to church camp here." That was something Juliet's father had won, after all. "Despite my mother's wish to turn us all into good little Presbyterians, my father was a French Catholic, and he insisted that his daughters would all be raised in the church."

"Have you ever been up there?"

"No." Warily she shook her head. "But there's so much to do. How do we get money for bail? What about—"

"Shh." Josh smiled, very slowly. "It's a perfect hike. We'll take an offering for Desi." He moved closer and took her hand. "For you, too, if you want."

Juliet looked up at him, at the breadth of his shoulders, the kindness of his deer eyes, and felt a squeezing in her heart that was both wonder and fear, hope and despair. "We'll see," she said. And although she wanted, in some ways, to leave her hand cradled in his, something bigger made her pull away. "Let's get my shoes. You can help me pick out good socks."

"All right."

She saw that she'd wounded him a little, but better a little wound now than a bigger one later. Despite her pleasure in his company, and her very real passion for him, there wasn't anything really alive inside of her to share, and he was right: he had a little girl to think about.

* * *

Juliet chose a pair of sturdy, lace-up boots that felt both warm and comfortable, along with thick woolen socks and something Josh called gaiters, a sort of thick nylon sock to tie over her jeans as they walked, to keep the snow out. Since she was there anyway, she also bought a good coat, much warmer than the one she'd brought from California. Who knew coats came with so many features? she thought happily, snuggling into it. Josh asked the girl in the shop if they could leave the old things there and pick them up on the way back, and she tucked them beneath the counter.

The jail was only a few blocks away, and they walked there after the trip to the store. The sergeant in control was pretty lax and let Desi come out to the table without handcuffs. Juliet gave her a paper cup of coffee she'd brought from the local coffee shop, flavored with vanilla and raw sugar, just the way Desi liked it.

Desi was not particularly open to being cheered up, however. She looked dull and distant, her face swollen as if she'd slept hard after crying hard. Her hair was in a braid, slightly mussed at the top. "You have to get me out of here," she said, and it seemed her voice came from somewhere deep in her chest. "I get panicky in that cell."

"There's no arraignment until Wednesday," Juliet said.

Desi narrowed her eyes. "That's not soon enough. You need to go see Judge Behrens, out on the County Line road and tell him what's going on. He'll get me out faster than that."

"Okay. We'll call him right away." Juliet touched her sister's hand. "Don't panic, honey. Just let it go. Everything is going to be okay."

"Is it?" Desi asked in a dull tone. She raised her eyes. "I didn't kill him, Juliet. I might have wanted to bash his head in. I might have been angry with him. But I wouldn't have shot him."

Juliet felt the beat of her hesitation went one half second too long. "I know," she said.

Desi raised her head and looked at her. She didn't say anything, just looked.

"I'm sorry," Juliet said. "I'm just worried about you."

Josh put his big hand on Desi's shoulder. "We'll get you out of here, babe."

She put her hand on top of his, looking worn and weary. "I know."

From outside came the sound of chanting. All three looked up and then the sergeant was in the room. "Sorry, you're gonna have to go back to your cell now."

"What's going on?" Desi lifted her chin. "Juliet, look and see."

But Josh was already across the room. "Protest," he said, "but I can't tell who or what. I think it has to do with you."

The sergeant nudged Desi along. "Come on," he said. "You need to get back in your cell before I get my ass in a sling."

"Yessir." She looked over her shoulder at Josh and Juliet. "Judge Behrens," she said. "Remember."

"We're on it," Josh said. "Don't worry."

Outside, it was plain that the anti-Desi contingent had organized the rally. A small knot of mostly women, led by a tall brunette in a yellow jacket, stood by the jail steps. Remember Claude Tsosie, a placard read. It showed a picture of Claude when he was a bit younger, and a reproduction of one of his paintings.

"What, he's a *political* cause now?" Juliet hissed to Josh as they came down the steps. She slowed, feeling an argument on her lips, but Josh took her arm.

He said gruffly, "Keep moving. The last thing we want is more attention brought to this whole thing."

Juliet glared at the brunette as they walked by, and the woman glared back, but they left it at that. "Let's make the phone call," Josh said, and stopped at a pay phone with a phone book on a metal cable. A tiny phone book, Juliet noticed. It was about the size of her address book back home.

Josh found the name and dialed it on his cell phone, and outlined the situation to the person on the other end. The judge obviously asked for clarification several times, and Josh offered facts. There was a short period of "yes," and "no" and "not that I know of."

Finally he said, "Thank you, Your Honor. Right. I'll call you later."

He hung up. "He's going to do what he can, he said. He thinks he can get her out on Monday, anyway."

"Good." Only two nights more. It was misery, Juliet knew, but it was better than a week or two or ten.

"Still want to hike?" Josh asked.

"Yes."

"Let's go." He'd brought a small day pack with him, and they headed straight west, to the box-end of the box canyon. Snow melted with dizzying speed, making pattering noises as it melted off the trees and ran into the creek. They crossed it on a little wooden bridge. When they got to the middle, Juliet had to stop to admire it for a moment—the blue-white snow piled up in the shadows, the rushing stream in its rocky bed, aspen coins gleaming through wherever the snow had melted. The air smelled of earth and pine and something elusive, that note that always said, simply, *mountains* to Juliet.

As she stood there, sunlight spilling over her head from that brilliant sky, something in her eased. "When we came here to camp, I loved that smell. I loved coming to camp," she said to Josh, breathing in the scent of the water. "Well, maybe not at first, because I was afraid, but I got to the point where I loved it. All three of us did. We always said we were going to grow up and come live here."

Josh said, "And Desi did it." He gestured up the sunny side of the canyon. "That way."

"And this is her home. I hate it that this has happened to her. She was so happy to be here."

"We're going to make this work. I promise."

They climbed on a gravel path, not terribly muddy, thanks to the gravel, but it was slippery enough Juliet was glad to have the hiking boots with their good tread. A signpost made of wood read simply, Shrine, 1.4 miles, and pointed the way.

"Do you think she killed Claude?" Josh asked.

Juliet jerked her gaze up to his face. "Do you?"

He pursed his lips. "Honestly, I don't know."

"Me, either," Juliet admitted. "The case against her is circumstantial, but it's a pretty strong circumstantial case."

"I do know that she will die if she goes to jail."

"I know. We have to get her out." Their feet crunched on the snow. "My gut says she didn't do it. That she might be really mad and she might have shot him if he'd tried to take something from the ranch, but I don't think she would ever kill anyone."

Josh took her hand. "We'll find the right guy."

She squeezed his hand. Let go. "Thank you."

"So, what did you like about camp, back in the day?"

"Everything." Juliet grinned. "Well, no, that's a lie. I loved a lot of things, but not all of it. There were a lot of bugs. I was afraid of the spiders in the cabins and the possibility of rattlesnakes and afraid of lightning and afraid of drowning in the lake." She gave him a rueful look. "Scaredy-Julie, that was me. Still is, I guess."

"You're not a scaredy-cat. You're brave. Very fierce, fighting for your sister."

"Really?" She looked at him.

He half chuckled. "You sound so surprised."

"We were supposed to find totem animals at camp. There was this whole process we went through, making a medicine bag, listening to the stories of the elders, writing down our dreams. There were even elders who came in from the Mariposa Utes, now that I think about it."

He nodded. "There's an education and outreach arm of the government. I'm sure that's who it was."

"Probably." Juliet flung her hair back from her face. "Well, we were all supposed to be open to animals who came to us, and I was so worried it was going to be something stupid for me, you know? Like a rabbit or something, all timid and shy."

"All animals have their places," he said.

"Yeah, but I'd had enough of being a rabbit. And there were my sisters—Desi was a wolf, surprise, surprise, and Miranda was a dragonfly, which is at least beautiful. But nothing came to me. I didn't have any dreams, didn't find feathers. I was a total failure at the whole vision quest thing."

He laughed.

"So, just before the end of the season, I was out in the woods and I found this skull and a claw. I was so excited and ran it back to camp to show my counselor who didn't really believe I'd found it, that somehow I'd planted it, because it was—ta da—a mountain lion."

"No kidding!"

Juliet shook her head. "No. Everybody was jealous and it seemed like a big joke because I really was so afraid of everything that a rabbit would have been a lot more accurate."

"But the mountain lion chose you."

"That's what the elder said. That your totem finds you."

"I see that lion medicine in you, Juliet."

"Thank you."

"Now you should be brave enough to let life in."

She paused. "I'd like to try."

"That's all a man can ask."

They walked along in the warming day, and Juliet noticed the most curious sense of well-being spreading through her. It had to do with the sunlight and the woods, the quiet and the birdcalls, the scent of pine trees and the scent of Josh. All of it. She liked it that they could walk together in silence, without having to fill it up with chatter. She liked the feeling of safety she had in his company, and the way he'd felt around her last night.

Sneaking a glance at his profile, she let that memory come rushing back through her, along her skin and the nape of her neck and the backs of her knees—he'd held her close all through the night. As if she were precious. As if she were beloved.

She'd never had that feeling before. It scared her.

And yet, she wasn't alone in risking things, was she. Tentatively, she reached out and slipped her hand into his. When he looked down, she gave him a little smile. His lips quirked slightly.

He didn't let go. They walked up and up, around a switchback and another, beneath aspens with fluttering leaf-coins spinning around over their heads, beneath pine groves, along open spaces where the snow from the night before had melted.

"What do you know about the shrine?" Josh asked.

"Not a lot, really. I know a lot of people come to see it, that there was some sort of miracle attached to it. Aren't there hiking tours that bring people to it in the summertime?"

"Yep. One path, actually, goes right over the corner of Desi's land."

"And what's the miracle?"

"There was a young girl—"

"Is there always?"

He grinned and related the story of a young girl who'd been born with club feet who promised the saint that she would walk to the falls if her feet could be transformed. It had taken her three days to make the trek, but she'd done it, and when she got there, ten thousand butterflies had swirled up out of their sleep and touched her all over. The girl was healed.

"And now," he continued, "every year, people make pilgrimages here, usually at a point of transition in their lives."

"That's beautiful."

He paused, catching his breath. "And now, we're here."

"Where?"

With a secret little smile, Josh led a few more steps and turned the corner, and the path dead-ended in a small, open meadow surrounded by trees.

"Oh, my!" Juliet sighed.

The shrine sat at the foot of a waterfall, which splashed into a hot springs that send up a steamy spray. A mist covered the ground in a thin layer. Stationed above the hot spring was the shrine, a large, old statue of the Virgin Mary, but not like any Juliet had ever seen. This one had the sweet, somehow robust face of a Guadalupe, with the lush, curvy body of a siren. Her arms were spread wide, and a faint smile curled up her lips. Flowers, real and artificial, were scattered at her feet, and a plethora of candles and candleholders stood in a sheltered little glass building, like a small greenhouse.

But most breathtaking were the butterflies. Thousands of them, attached to the trees and rocks in a thousand different ways; butterflies made of cloth and embroidered with beads and braided out of ribbons; painted and carved and fashioned from rocks; tiny and large. Expressions of gratitude and petitions for intercession. For a moment, stunned into silence, Juliet thought she could hear whispers, of praises, prayer, petition, thanksgiving.

"It's so beautiful!" she cried.

"In the summertime, there are thousands of mourning cloak butterflies," he said. "It's unbelievable."

"What do they look like?"

"They're black, with a little ribbon of yellow around the edges of their wings, and a blue spot on each wing."

Just then, as if called by his description, a butterfly looped upward on a warm draft from the hot springs, its wings shimmery and beautiful.

"How is that *possible?*" Julie cried.

"They can last over the winter," Josh said. "Hold out your hand."

"I'm afraid! It'll feel weird!"

"It's half asleep. They have to warm up their wings before they can fly."

"No, no. You do it."

He chuckled and extended his hand. The butterfly lazily circled and landed on his finger, wings working. "Now you," he said. "Hold out your hand."

Juliet obeyed. The creature swooped and landed, as if a benevolent spirit were visiting, and to her surprise, she felt some intense, unnamed emotion rise in her throat. "It's beautiful!" she whispered, afraid to so much as breathe for fear it would fly away again. So close, she could see butterfly eyes and the pattern of scales on his wings and the long feelers.

Amazing.

In a moment, it lifted off and swirled lazily upward, as if carrying prayers toward heaven. Juliet swallowed. She didn't meet Josh's eye as she moved forward, and took a candle from the box by the little housing. Josh stepped away and Juliet was grateful for the privacy as she lit the candle and put it inside the safe house. Looking up at the sweet face of the saint, she whispered an urgent prayer. "Let her get through this safely. Please."

After a moment, Josh came forward. "My turn," he said, and Juliet gave him the same privacy. As she stood beneath the trees, waiting, she couldn't help but sneak a small glance backward at him, at his tall, sturdy frame, his walnut-colored skin, his beautiful cheekbones. An arrow went through her chest—*I'm falling in love with him!*—and then she turned away.

He came up behind her. "Are you ready to go back to town? I'm going to have to get Glory home pretty soon."

"Sure." She looked at the heavily dripping snow. "I wonder if I should go up to the cabin tonight. It looks like it will be fine up there, doesn't it?"

He met her eyes. "I can take you if you like, but the cabin is above 9000 feet. There will be a lot more snow up there than there is down here."

"You're the expert." She cleared her throat. "I was thinking, in part, of Glory. Like giving her the wrong idea."

"It'll be all right." He raised his chin, scanned the horizon. "It's not like we're all over each other or anything."

Again she had the sense that his feelings were

wounded. There was a faint stiffness around his jaw and mouth. "Josh, I'm not sure what—"

"Don't worry about it, all right?"

Stung, she said, "Fine."

Josh was aware of a knot in his chest the size of Montana as they went through the rest of their errands. They stopped in the drugstore so that Juliet could get some hair rollers, then by the store where they'd stashed their things from earlier. Only then did they walk to Helene's house to pick up Glory.

His mother had obviously been cooking, and the house smelled of her trademark corn fritters and potato soup. She came out, wiping her hands on a cup towel, rangy and lean, and not at all a grandmotherly-looking sort. "Hello, Juliet!" she cried. "What a nice surprise."

Josh bent down and kissed his mother's cheek, handed her a bag of supplies, and called out, "Glory, I'm here!"

"I'm looking at a book right now!" she yelled from the kitchen.

Helene lifted an eyebrow. "She might not have had as much sleep as usual, spending the night with her friend."

"We're gonna have a talk about that," Josh said gruffly.

"No, we are not," his mother replied serenely. "You're too protective. Time to lighten up."

"Glory!" Josh yelled. "I brought somebody who knows how to curl hair."

"She wants her hair curled?" Helene asked. "Why didn't she ask me?"

"Because you have *short* hair, Grandma!" Glory

said, coming out of the kitchen. She carried a book, with her fingers stuck between two pages. She would be five in six weeks, and he was pretty sure she had taught herself to read quite some time ago, but she pretended she didn't know how if anyone asked. She always said was just looking at the pictures with Pink and Ink.

"Silly me," Helene said, plucking at her thick, cropped hair. "I still know how to curl hair."

"I've never seen you with a curl."

"True." Helene waved a hand good-naturedly.

Glory had not caught sight of Juliet yet. Juliet waited by the door, looking oddly nervous, her mittened hands smushed together. As Josh looked at her, his senses were slammed again, a winding depth of memory, yearning, desire, braided together. Her lips were a little swollen from their kissing last night, and he only had to look at her to remember the way she tasted, when they'd—

"Princess!" Glory squealed. "Hi!"

"Hey, sweetheart." Her low, well-modulated voice poured like butter into the room. "I'm so happy to see you."

"You haven't been to my grandma's house before! Are *you* going to curl my hair?"

Juliet smiled and held up a plastic bag from the grocery store. "I've got the rollers right here."

"Can we do it right now?"

"Wait until you wash your hair, kiddo," Josh said. "After supper. Juliet is going to stay with us until tomorrow because she's not used to being all alone in the mountains, and Desi is—" He scowled "—away for the weekend."

"You're going to stay in *my house?*" Glory said.

"Just for tonight, if that's okay?"

"Yes! We can read stories, maybe. Or if you want, we could watch *Snow White* or *Cinderella* or—" she leaned on Josh's leg "—what other ones do I have?"

Her face was awash with light and excitement. Josh put his hand on her silky head. "We have a lot of DVDs," he said. "I'm sure we can find one to watch together."

Juliet looked up, and he saw for the first time the slight bruising beneath her eyes, the weariness and strain of the past few days starting to show. "I'm really looking forward to it."

"First, we're going to eat some of the best corn fritters you've ever tasted," Josh said, and picked his daughter up. "Who makes the best?"

Glory raised her hands above her head, a cheerleader move. "Grandma!"

"It's not ready for a little while," Helene said. "Maybe another twenty minutes on the soup."

"No problem." Josh wiggled Glory in his arms. "Whatcha want to do?"

"Wash my hair."

"Then we'd have to go home with it wet. Not a good idea." He shook his head sadly. "Your hair would turn into icicles and fall on the ground and break into pieces. Not great."

"Na-uh!" She narrowed her eyes suspiciously. "That sounds like a story."

"Let's go read the book, kiddo."

"Okay. You want to read with us, Princess?"

Josh spoke up before Juliet had a chance. "The princess is going to hang out with Grandma."

"I am?"

He nodded firmly. When she just stood there, awkwardly holding the bag of drugstore hair rollers and barrettes and such things, he took it from her, nudged her shoulder. "Go on in there and sit at the table, Princess. I'm going to let you borrow my mom for a little while."

As Juliet stripped off her coat and sat down at the big wooden table in Helene's roomy kitchen, she suddenly felt exhausted. Not just a little bit tired, or stressed, but absolutely, bone-deep demolished. Everything seemed to catch up with her at once—Desi's arrest, the emotional storm from last night, the sudden and surprising connection to Josh and all that stirred up. Not to mention all the purely physical things they'd been doing—hiking, making love, walking all over town.

"You look all done in, honey," Helene said, touching her hair. "Can I get you a cup of tea?"

"That would be wonderful."

From the doorway, Josh said, "Ma, remember my friend Agatha, from the Ute School?"

"Sure."

Josh looked at Juliet, significantly. Nodded.

Juliet scowled. "Don't make secret gestures around me," she said irritably.

He half grinned. "The princess needs a nap."

Helene shooed him out of the kitchen. "He's my one and only," she confessed as she poured water into a red enameled teakettle. "I might have spoiled him a little. He thinks he knows what's best for everybody all the time."

Juliet couldn't even muster up much of a smile. She nodded, was caught by a massive yawn, and covered her mouth. "Sorry! We hiked up to the shrine so I could light a candle for Desi. I think I'm pretty tired."

"Have you seen your sister this morning?"

"Yeah. She's not doing well."

Helene said, "She's a wolf—jail will kill her. We have to make sure she gets out. We're going to drum for her tonight, her sisters and I."

"Sisters?"

"Spiritual sisters, I guess you'd call it. We sweat together. To heal ourselves, each other, the earth."

Juliet could think of nothing to say to that. "I see."

"Maybe you'd like to come sometime."

"Maybe." She wasn't sure what it entailed and it seemed a little bit intimidating.

"You can think about it." Helene sat at the table, her kind, strong face as calm as a mountain morning. Her hands, long-fingered and graceful, were very much like her son's, and she folded them in front of her the same way. "I am a healer, Juliet. May I take your hands?"

"Um. Okay." Juliet put her hands on the table, and Helene enfolded them in her own. Her fingertips were cool at first, but as she held Juliet's hands in her own, Helene's hands warmed up, getting hotter and hotter with every passing second. When it seemed it would be uncomfortable and Juliet would have to pull away, the heat suddenly stabilized and Juliet let go of a breath.

"You're worn out," Helene said.

Juliet nodded. She had a sudden vision of herself crawling into a cave and curling up by a fire to sleep and sleep and sleep. Hibernating.

"Winter," Helene said, her voice sounding more lyrical somehow, "is the time we can rest. Sleep more, eat more. Like the earth, we're being more quiet. You can use this winter to let all those wounds heal, and by spring, you'll feel much better."

Juliet thought about saying, "I'm not wounded," but it would have been such a blatant lie that she would shame herself uttering it aloud. Instead she heard herself say, "I lost my job a month ago. I worked so hard to get it, and then—"

"Then?"

She dropped her gaze. It wasn't that she didn't want to say anything more; it was that she couldn't seem to focus on just one thing to pull out and offer as an explanation. *I was raped* seemed as valid as *I am not sure that was ever what I wanted. I think my mother wanted it for me.*

Finally she said, "I don't know. I don't seem to want to do anything to get it back. It doesn't matter. Or—it matters, but it's not *my* job." Which sounded stupid, so she added, "Or something like that." Frowning, she said, "That doesn't make any sense."

"It makes a lot of sense. Maybe there's something else you need to do now."

Juliet thought of the mothers she'd met at the immigrant center, both earnest and weary, with their children clinging to their legs. How satisfying it had been to help them find work, housing, food for another day or two! "The law doesn't move very fast," she said. "I was growing more and more frustrated with the way that worked in people's lives."

Helene nodded. Patiently, she kept her hands around Juliet's, her eyes steady and calm, her face smooth. "What brought it to a head?"

"I was raped," Juliet said simply. "A year ago."

No ripple of judgment or shock or slightly prurient interest. Helene simply nodded. A quiet radiance came from her, and it felt like it was spreading to Juliet, a silvery energy that radiated upward from her hands, through her arms, into her tight, weary shoulders.

She would have said she didn't believe in hands-on healing, but it was impossible to deny there was something going on with Helene's hands. It was pleasant enough she didn't feel the need to do anything about it. For long moments, they simply sat at the table, her small hands enfolded in Helene's larger, rangier ones.

The kettle began to whistle. Gently, Helene pressed Juliet's hands together. "Let me get the tea."

As she poured water into the kettle, Juliet asked, "What happened to Josh's friend at the Ute School?"

"She was abandoned by her mother."

"Oh." Juliet felt a ripple pulse through her, a sense of having been recognized, seen. Josh hadn't focused on the rape at all, but on her feelings of not being able to reach her mother. It took her breath for a moment.

Why did people fall in love? Was that what was happening here? And if it was, why was Juliet so skittish?

Somewhere in the house, a phone rang. "Uh-oh," Helene said. That's Josh's phone. Usually means trouble."

Josh looked grim when he came into the kitchen a few

minutes later. "That was my friend on the sheriff's department, who called earlier to let me know they got a search warrant to go through the cabin for possible evidence."

"They can get a search warrant but they can't get a bail hearing?" Juliet asked with annoyance. "What *is* that?"

"They took her rifle and some clothes, maybe some other things." He touched his nose with his thumb again, that thinking gesture. "The ballistics test was inconclusive."

"That's good, right?"

"It doesn't clear her," Josh said gravely. "The bad news is, they found Claude's blood on some of her clothes."

Chapter 14

For one long second, Juliet couldn't breathe as the reality of Josh's words sank in. *They found Claude's blood on some of Desi's clothes.*

It made her dizzy. A thousand scenarios played out in the space of moments—Desi in prison, ankles chained, eyes hollow with despair, the wolves euthanized one by one, the land turning into a retreat for the very, very rich. She made a noise of protest and covered her eyes. "Dang it."

"If you have any high-powered criminal lawyer contacts," Josh said, "This would be a good time to call them."

With an ironic twist of her lips, she said, "My old boyfriend. Who probably isn't talking to me."

"Call him," Josh said.

Juliet glared at him. "You have a bad habit of ordering people around, you know that? I'm not a child and I'm not one of your minions on the police force, and if you want something from me, you need to ask politely."

Helene grinned.

Josh took a breath. His eyes glittered suddenly as he gazed down at her, and his tongue laced out and touched his lower lip. To her amazement, the sight of that healthy pink tongue, the tip that had given so much pleasure, the plumpness of lower lip, gave her a jolt of yearning.

He took a step closer. "Yes, ma'am," he drawled, a country boy without guile. "Your sister needs a lawyer. A very good lawyer. Do you have any contacts you can lean on?"

"Better." She raised her chin. "I just might." Taking her phone out of her bag, she flipped it open and punched in a number. "Alicia," she said to the voice mail of her friend, "this is Juliet Rousseau. My sister is in criminal trouble in Colorado and we might need the names of some good lawyers here. Give me a call when you can, on my cell phone."

"Good work," Josh said as she hung up.

She found herself preening just the tiniest bit. "Thanks."

After feasting on soup and fritters, Josh, Juliet and Glory walked through the gilded late afternoon to Josh's house. The dogs had been romping the fenced backyard all day and were very happy to see the humans arrive. They set up howls of greeting as they stepped onto the porch.

Nothing would do but Glory had to have her hair washed and set right now, and Josh excused himself to make phone calls, promising to see what he could find out, how much information he could gather from various sources.

Meanwhile, Juliet let the very female pleasure of giving Glory a bath and washing her hair take away the sting and worry of the day. Dozens of toys were collected in a laundry basket by the big bathtub, and Glory picked out a few to toss in the tub as Juliet started the water and adjusted it. "Do you want bubbles?"

"No, then I can't see my toys."

Juliet chuckled. "Ah." She started humming under her breath, stirring the water around to make sure it was the right temperature, and she unlaced Glory's braid. Her hair was thick and cool and elegant, and Juliet luxuriated in the feeling of it, spilling over her hands. "You have very, very pretty hair," she said.

"I got it from my daddy." Glory stripped out of her clothes and gingerly stepped into the tub. "My mommy has really yellow hair."

"She does?"

"It was really supposed to be black, but she didn't like being Indian."

"Oh, I'm sure she did," Juliet said.

"No. She told me she didn't." Matter-of-factly, Glory filled a cup with water from the running tap and poured it into a bowl. "I like being Indian."

"I'm glad."

"My Daddy says I look like Pocahontas. Do you think I do?"

"Absolutely. Do you have that movie on DVD?"

"Yeah! You want to watch that one with me tonight?"

"Sure."

The smell of the soap and the shampoo, the easy pleasure of sitting on the closed lid of the toilet, making small talk with a little girl, made Juliet feel peaceful. She washed Glory's back, then her hair, and rinsed it with detangler, and helped her out into a big, fluffy turquoise towel. When Glory was dressed in her footed pajamas—pink, of course, with little kittens all over them—Juliet led her into the living room to sit by the fire, where she brushed Glory's hair to get it mostly dry before she put it on the rollers. Josh's voice came from the kitchen in low tones, only the odd word coming through here and there.

"My sister has very long pretty hair," Juliet said. "We use to brush each other's hair all the time."

"So does Pink," Glory said. "But hers is red."

"Who is Pink?"

"She's my friend. Not like Natasha at school. Pink and Ink are in my room. Or if I want, they'll come along in my pocket."

"I see. Like imaginary friends?"

"Sometimes, grown-ups pretend they can see them, but I know they can't." Glory held very still as Juliet rolled the first section of hair into a curler. "Grown-ups can't see angels anymore, can they?"

"I guess not." Juliet secured the roller, and picked up another section. In front of them, the fire crackled and snapped. Two dogs—Crazy Horse and Tecumseh, snored nearby, tuckered out by their long day playing outside. "Pink and Ink are angels?"

"Yeah. Pink is a girl and Ink is a boy. They were brother and sister before they died and went to heaven. They came to take care of me when my mommy stole me." Glory gave Juliet a long-suffering look that was well beyond her years. "My mommy wasn't very good at taking care of me."

Juliet had a sense, suddenly, that Josh was listening. "So, how did Pink and Ink help you?"

"A lot of ways! They showed me how to get on the counter so I could get some cheese and bread. They showed me how to lock the door when I was all by myself."

"Really! All that. Very good angels."

"Yeah," she said with a shrug. "They are. I mostly liked it when I was scared and they came and slept with me. Grandma says they're my spirit guides and when I get older, they'll be the ones to help me find out what I'm gonna do when I get big."

Josh ambled into the room, deceptively casual, and sat on the couch. "I never knew that, about Pink and Ink," he said. "They took care of you?"

"They always take care of me, Daddy. You know that."

"I do?"

"Yeah. You said your prayers, so God sent angels to watch over me."

Over Glory's head, Juliet met Josh's eyes. If only, she thought, it was that simple. And yet, hadn't she gone this morning to light candles for Desi?

Josh looked stricken. "So I did, honey. So I did."

"Can we watch *Pocahontas?*" she asked.

"I'd love to." He looked at Juliet. "Suit you, too?"

She nodded. When all the rollers were in place, Juliet dried the curls with a blow dryer, then let them out and curls fell in beautiful ringlets over Glory's shoulders.

Juliet couldn't help but grin. Glory looked like a vision of an angel, or a Victorian drawing.

"Wow, kiddo," Josh said. "You sure do have a lot of hair."

Glory stood for a long time in front of the bedroom mirror, the only one she could see into without help or standing on something. She flipped her hair over her shoulder, smoothed her hands over it, walked very close to the mirror and nodded. "I look pretty," she said.

"You definitely do," Juliet agreed, and wondered when girls lost the ability to do that—announce she looked good without hemming and hawing about it.

They all piled together on the couch, Glory sandwiched between the two adults. Tecumseh came and pushed himself beneath Juliet's feet, slumping happily asleep with her feet on his side. Jack, Josh's dog, whined until Josh let him up on the couch. Crazy Horse, not to be left out, curled up close by.

It was slightly overwhelming, Juliet thought. It was warm. It made her feel loved and protected.

And the way Glory held her hand, and kept looking up at her as if to be sure she was really there, made her realize she had to be very, very careful with this little girl's heart.

After Glory was settled in bed, her new curls protected with a scarf, Juliet took her phone out of her purse and held it for a long minute before she flipped it open and dialed Scott's number. It rang in her ear, then his voice mail picked up. "It's Juliet. My sister is in trouble and I could use some advice if you are not too annoyed with me."

She hung up and looked at Josh, sitting in his chair, whittling with an expression of deep concentration. "That's that, I guess."

He nodded. All evening he'd been very cool and distant, and Juliet had put it down to keeping things cool in front of Glory. But there was no Glory around now, and he was still locked tight inside his own little world.

"What do we do now?" Juliet asked. Nudging him.

"Wait. Watch television. Read a book. Knit."

"Oh, sure. I have my knitting right here."

He shrugged. "I'm thinking about what Glory said about Pink and Ink, protecting her. That was pretty wild, wasn't it?"

"What a survivor she is, your daughter!"

"What do you mean?"

"She found a way at—what, four?—to get her needs met. She created a world where she had help when she needed it."

"I didn't think of it like that."

"I don't think you have to worry about her, Josh. I think she's fine."

"Really?"

"Really." She touched his hand. "She's a great kid."

He leaned back on the couch. "She is that. I'm worried that she worships you."

"Me, too. She asked me to marry you the first day."

He grinned, showing those big white teeth. "You didn't tell me that."

"Pretty funny."

"It is." Josh took her hand, worried her fingers. "The other thing on my mind tonight is the blood on Desi's clothes." He shook his head. "It's a nightmare. If they can put her at the scene—and even if they can't, it's well known she was chasing the mountain lion that mauled him—then there's not a damned thing we can do about it."

"I have to keep believing it's going to work out," Juliet said. "Don't you dare give up yet."

"I'm not giving up. I'm talking to you as a cop. This is bad."

The doorbell rang and Josh scowled, then put down the wooden block and stood up to answer it. Juliet heard voices, then Josh returned with another man behind him—the bartender from the Black Crown, the pub they'd visited last night.

Something about him was jovial and upbeat, even under such gruesome circumstances. "Hello" he said, "you're Juliet, isn't that right?" His accent was the slightly drawling New Zealand British.

"Yep." She stood. "Was it Tam? How are you?"

"I heard some gossip I thought might help you."

Josh gestured toward the couch. "Have a seat. Want a beer or something?"

"No, thank you." He settled on the couch, laced his fingers together. "I've been seeing a woman who—" he tsked, inclined his head "—might be a bit of a gold digger. Not looking at me, 'course, though I've got the pub, it's not on the order of the payoff she's lookin' to find, you understand."

"Not uncommon around here."

Juliet widened her eyes. "Really?"

"Just wait, sweetheart, for the ski season to get going." His sentences ended on questions. "You'll see what we mean."

"So, the one you've been seeing?" Josh prompted.

"Right. Elsa." He looked at his palms. "She's Norwegian, a beauty and after a rich man. There's a developer in the pub who's promising her the moon and more, and he was talking this afternoon about how the land with the wolves will be so much better spent as a spa."

"Not sure what that proves."

"Nothing, mate. But it's gossip. Could help."

Josh nodded, his mouth grim. "Have you heard other developers speculating about the land?"

He lifted a finger. "I have, and it's better." His pale green eyes had a directness Juliet found appealing. "There's some talk of an enclosed aquifer, a hot spring, beneath the wolf center."

Josh straightened. He let go of a long, low whistle.

"Just rumor," Tam said. "But worth mentioning."

"I don't understand why that would be a big deal," Juliet said.

"It could be tapped for energy," Josh said. "Steam heat that can be recycled back into the earth. Theoretically, it's an eternal energy source."

"Worth billions, likely," Tam added.

"Wow."

Josh nodded. "She made the deal of the century with that land, I'm telling you."

"She really did." Juliet pressed a hand to her diaphragm. "It scares me."

"The good news is," Josh said, "it's a lot of motive for murder, and to frame Desi. That's what we need right now."

"Yes," she said. "Thanks, Tam."

He winked. "No problem."

Tam left and for the second time in two nights, Josh brought the quilts and pillows out to the couch. Last night, when he had returned with the pillows, Juliet had lit candles and built up the fire, an invitation in her eyes. Tonight, when he returned, she'd tumbled sideways, clutching a pillow, and stared at the fire with a melancholy expression.

"You look like you've lost your best friend," he said, settling beside her. With an easy gesture, he rubbed her arm.

"Long day." She looked at him. "Thanks for all your help."

"You're welcome."

They sat there. The fire crackled. Her cheek, curved and white, invited his fingers, and Josh resisted. Her throat, long and smooth, invited his lips, and he resisted. "I guess this is…uh…good night."

"Okay." She shifted to look at him. "It's awkward, Josh, but this is probably the right decision for now. With Glory and all the stuff with Desi and—"

He kissed her, cutting her off. He didn't even know

he was going to do it until he was bending over her, claiming that lush and seductive mouth.

And if she had resisted, if she had protested or pulled away, he would have respected that and taken himself off to bed.

But she didn't. With a little cry, she met his kiss and flung her arms around his neck, pulling him close to her. They had been slow in previous times and easy with each other. Josh had been mindful of her wariness, and she'd had a fragile way about her that was tentative and quiet.

Not now. It was as if their kiss let free the tigers of hunger and yearning and need that had been circling all day. Her mouth opened wide, inviting the hard, fierce thrust of his tongue; her hands laced into his hair tightly and pulled him close.

"Not here," Josh murmured, and picked her up and carried her, easily, into his bedroom, where they shed their clothes in a tangle and a tumble, tossing them wherever they landed until both were naked, and shivering and Josh drove himself home between her thighs, into slick heat and quivering warmth and the surprising strength of her grip.

And when they were spent, they were both so worn from the long day that they simply curled together.

"We can't keep doing this," Juliet said thickly, her head nestled against his chest.

"I know." He pressed a kiss to her hair.

But they would. He'd finally understood a simple truth about Juliet Rousseau. It wasn't only her feelings about the rape that were buried, it was her feelings about everything. He held her, quietly, and thought about the things she'd said about her mother. "I think you need to tell your mother what happened to you, Juliet."

"Why?"

"Because I think you need to confess it to her."

"Confess? Like a sin?"

"No," he said quietly, brushing hair from her forehead. "Like a sorrow."

"She won't understand."

"It doesn't matter. It's not for her. It's for you."

Her hand moved on his chest, slow and easy, as if she was drawing comfort from the feeling of his skin. "I'll think about it."

"Will you also consider a support group?"

She was very quiet for a long stretch. "I don't know. We'll see."

They fell asleep, naked and exhausted, in each other's arms.

After breakfast, Juliet went to see Desi at the jail. If possible, Desi looked even worse, her skin the color of gruel, her hair unbrushed. Juliet hugged her, tightly. "Don't give up on me, Desi. Josh talked to the judge yesterday and he thinks you can be out tomorrow morning."

Desi nodded dully. "I had so many dreams last night. That mountain lion is haunting me. I swear I heard him last night."

"Do you want me to call somebody?"

She shook her head. "No, there's nothing they can

do until he shows up somewhere. I just hate that he's in pain for so long. There was a lot of blood out at the ranch."

"Is there anything you want? Anything I can do?"

Desi roused herself to give Juliet a wan smile. "Just watch out for my dogs."

"That I can do." She paused. "Desi, can I talk about something kind of frivolous?"

"Please," she said, sipping the latte Juliet had brought to her.

"I broke up with Scott."

"You did? When?"

"Right after I met Josh." She bit her lip. "The thing is, I just can't seem to get to my feelings. Not any of them. I mean, I think I was very attracted to Josh and that's what made me realize that Scott and I were just drifting. But then Josh kisses me and I can feel things while his hands are on me, but the minute I move away, it's like a wall snaps into place."

"I'm glad you broke up with Scott, first of all. I never liked him. He was too uptight."

Juliet smiled. "I know."

"And Josh—well, if I were to pick any man in the world for you, I couldn't do better than him. But you're going to have to do your healing work or nothing is ever going to be okay again."

Juliet took a breath and confessed her secret. "I don't know how."

"Just be with it," Desi said. A little color came back into her cheeks as she counseled her sister. "When you're afraid, just be afraid. When you're mad, be mad. You don't always have to be the good girl."

The advice held a stinging rightness. Juliet nodded. "I'll try."

"That's all anyone can do."

Chapter 15

Josh drove her home in the late afternoon, at Juliet's request. After her conversation with Desi, Juliet knew that her instinct to stay alone and face her mostly insubstantial fears was a good one. If all went well, Desi would get out of jail tomorrow morning—this would be a chance for Juliet to spend one night alone in the mountains.

It worried her a little that there was more snow in the forecast, but there were plenty of supplies, and she wouldn't even technically be alone, after all; the dogs would be with her. Josh went through the cabin with her, made sure she understood how the various things worked, and he carried in several armloads of firewood for her, not listening when she protested that she knew how to do it. "I know you do. It doesn't hurt to take some help, either."

At last, he paused at the front door. "You don't have to do this," he said. "There's nothing to prove."

Juliet nodded. "Yes, there is. I need to prove to myself that I'm not going to be afraid forever."

He seemed as if he would say something else, then just shrugged. "Okay. Call me if you need me."

As the mountain darkness enveloped the cabin, Juliet determined to keep herself busy. She boiled pasta and grated cheddar for macaroni and cheese while she listened to Celtic tunes on her MP3 player. While the macaroni and cheese baked, she tidied up the cabin, which took all of six minutes, since they had not been there the past couple of days. The fire was going nicely in the potbellied stove, and she had already piled up her nest of pillows and quilts so she could read after dinner.

One of the dogs went outside, then another, then the last one, but Juliet didn't fret. The blackness of the uncurtained windows was bothersome, as always, and Juliet wondered with some annoyance why Desi had never made any curtains.

Well, aside from the fact that you didn't technically need them since there were no neighbors, save for the odd bear.

And the views were spectacular.

Still, at night, it was creepy to know anyone else could see inside and she couldn't see out.

Anyone else being who, exactly? a voice in her mind asked. The odd werewolf, the rapist who had followed her from California to here to rape her again in the high mountains in an isolated cabin that no one knew existed?

Something like that. Vampires, rapists, crazed serial killers.

She rolled her eyes at the absurdity of her thoughts and wished she could turn on the television for company. That was how she got through the loneliness and fear back home—she turned on the television and let the chatter and advertisements and constant, on-demand companionship blunt the terror she felt, the sense of her own isolation, even in the midst of a big city. She had done it as a child, too, taken refuge in the world of game shows, soap operas, movie of the week. Her mother had disapproved, but it kept Juliet out of her hair, so she looked the other way.

The bell on the stove dinged and Juliet took out a small, beautiful casserole, the top lightly browned. As if she called them, the dogs all reappeared, sitting politely along an imaginary line Desi had drawn for them as if to say, "Are we not the best dogs you've ever seen?"

Juliet chuckled. "You are great dogs and I will have some treats for you in a little while."

She set the table and ate supper, reading the novel she'd started before Desi's arrest. It was enjoyable enough. The wind started to blow outside, and a little while after that, it started to snow lightly. The silence was vast, apart from the wind that blasted against the window panes every so often. When she'd finished her macaroni and cheese, she gave the waiting dogs the leftovers and they took them politely, delicately, as Desi had taught them.

Desi. Juliet carried the dishes to the sink and thought about her sister. And the one thing Juliet was most afraid of was that Desi really had killed Claude. Her blood on his clothes. The inconclusive ballistics report, the fury Desi had been feeling.

Be with whatever you're feeling.

Juliet's eye twitched as she thought of other things: Desi's desire to kill Juliet's rapist, the fact that Desi could not account for her whereabouts that night.

A night Juliet had spent alone, now that she thought about it. The difference had been that she hadn't realized she was alone. She thought she'd only be by herself for a few hours, and she had dogs to protect herself.

She and the dogs padded over to the stove and settled into the nest. Juliet pulled the quilts around herself, propped up against the wall with pillows, and stared into the fire, dancing yellow and orange against the gloom.

Desi had always been unlike other women. She was stronger, tougher, smarter. She strode through the world like some ancient goddess, the hunter Diana with her dogs. She'd been bolder, fiercer than her sisters, traveling boldly, learning things like how to hunt and fire a rifle. She'd gone to the Peace Corps, moved to the mountains, started a sanctuary for wolves.

Unlike anyone else.

Juliet's throat felt tight as she imagined the disaster awaiting Desi if it turned out she really had killed a worthless scumbag of a man, a charmer and a user who'd taken advantage of entirely too many women over the years.

No.

She didn't, in her heart, believe Desi had done it. Which meant someone else had. Which meant Juliet just had to find out who. In the morning, she would go talk to the girlfriend, and see about any other girlfriends who might have something to share. The one thing Juliet was good at was talking to women, even hostile women. Why hadn't she thought of this before?

Because she'd been too busy being afraid, focusing on fear and all the terrible things that could happen instead of all the good. She thought of Glory's faith, the angels who had protected her through a dark time, the angels that had brought her home safely to her father.

Where had her own faith gone? Juliet wondered now. Had it been so fragile it could be demolished by a single person with an evil agenda?

Her cell phone rang, and startled one of the dogs, who barked wildly for a minute. Juliet laughed and rubbed his head. "It's okay, silly. It's just a phone." She flipped it open and said, "Hello?"

"Hi, Juliet." It was Josh, his voice like dark toffee.

She let the sound of her smile enter her voice. "Hey, Josh. What's up?"

"I was just thinking about you and thought I'd give you a call."

"Yeah? Were you worrying?"

"No."

"Good." She twisted a piece of hair around her index finger, leaning back more comfortably on the pillows. "Because you really don't need to. I'm having some pretty deep thoughts up here."

"Am I interrupting?"

"No, actually," she said in a more serious tone. "You're part of what I'm thinking about."

"You're thinking about my parts?"

Juliet laughed. "I am. Big, juicy parts."

"Me, too."

A softness of silence fell between them. The fire crackled and the wind blew and the dogs snored. In her mind was his angled face, his thick dark hair. "I was thinking, honestly, about how safe I feel around you. I don't know that I've ever had that feeling before, with anyone, and it's kind of weird."

"Is it bad to feel safe?"

"No. I'm just not used to it."

"Well, you make me feel the opposite of safe, Juliet. I've been pretty well protected, and you slammed right by my walls. Like they weren't even there. I'm worried about that."

"Worried why?"

"Because you have a whole life in L.A., not here. Because you're a city girl and that's who screwed up my life last time. Because my daughter thinks you hung the moon and she doesn't need to get hurt again and I don't know how to protect her from it."

"The truth is, Josh, you can't." Juliet rubbed her foot along the back of a dog. "The world isn't safe. Not for any of us."

"I know. But you can cut the risks."

"Maybe." Juliet paused. "I am a girly girl, by the way, not a city girl. There's a difference."

He chuckled, the sound low and warm. "I stand corrected." He fell silent again, and Juliet was surprised by how much she liked knowing he was there, just on the other end of the phone. "It's not all that easy for me to talk about feelings, Juliet, but you're not like anyone I've ever met. It's like you smell right or something."

"I know what you mean," she said, and realized that she'd been breaking up with Scott in her mind within minutes of meeting Josh. The look of him, the sound of him—even, yes, the smell of him. But it was something deeper than physical, something unnamable, a recognition. "I felt like—" She realized she'd been about to say something really stupid and halted. "Never mind."

"Come on, be dopey with me, huh? If the girl doesn't start, the guy can never go there."

"Okay. I felt like I'd known you before," she said.

"Good," Josh said. "Me, too."

In the distance, a wolf howled, and then another. The dogs, apparently comatose up to that moment, sat up, ears pricked to alertness. Another round of howling went up, a series of yips and yowls that made the hair on Juliet's neck rise.

"Hold on," she said, and put the phone down to her chest, dancing over to the window to see if there was an animal in view.

"Sorry," she said, coming back on. "The wolves are going nuts up there."

"Might be an animal," Josh said.

"What kind of an animal?"

"I don't know. A bear. A deer. A mountain lion. It is the mountains, you know."

"A bear? Yikes."

"If it worries you, give Alex a call, see if he's seen anything."

"Good idea, thank you." She paused. "I guess I'll talk to you tomorrow, then, all right?"

Tecumseh jumped up and padded over to the window, where he went absolutely still, then growled at something he saw.

"Uh-oh."

Tecumseh bolted for the dog door in the back of the kitchen. Juliet didn't hesitate—she dropped the phone and ran for the door, trying to get there before Tecumseh bolted through. "Damn it!"

Desi would never forgive her if something happened to these dogs. She was seconds too late—jamming her index finger in the process, eating dog fur as she slammed into the door. "Damn!" she cried.

The other two dogs, alerted, leapt to their feet, nails skittering on the floor as they, too, bolted for the dog door to see what the commotion was all about. Tecumseh followed on Sitting Bull's heels before she could stop him. She managed to tackle Crazy Horse before he got out, yelling "no!" as authoritatively as she could manage. Before he got out, she flipped the lock—then felt immediately guilty. What if they needed to retreat by coming back inside?

But while the other two were easily wolves when it came to the hunt, Crazy Horse was more of a dog, and she didn't want him hurt.

In the distance, the wolves howled and cried in an eerie cacophony of sound. Closer in, she didn't hear the other dogs, but Crazy Horse dashed for the window and whined, a low, eerie sound that made the hair on her neck stand up. "Come on, baby," she said, taking him by the collar and leading him into the bathroom. He wasn't happy about it when she closed the door, barking in protest, but she needed to think about what to do.

Back in the living room, she turned off the lights and peered out the window. The dogs were nowhere in view. The night was cloudy, and very dark—impossible to see anything.

Something yipped, a sound like an animal in pain. One of the dogs. Damn! Juliet instinctively ran for the cabinet where Desi kept the guns. The only thing left was a handgun, but there was a box of bullets right beside it, and when she looked at it, it looked like it had bullets in it.

From her cell phone on the floor came a tinny voice. "Juliet! What's going on?"

She dove for the phone, picked it up. "Josh, it's okay. There's an animal out there, the dogs are freaking out. How do I shoot a gun if I need to?"

"Holy Mother of God," he breathed. "What kind of gun?"

"Handgun, pistol. I don't know. It's heavy. It has bullets in it."

Another pained animal sound, and Juliet whirled around, wishing she had x-ray vision to see what was out there. A bear? A coyote?

"I'm here. I've gotta do something." Without waiting for an answer, she dashed for the dog door and flung the lock open, whistling for Sitting Bull and Tecumseh. Sitting Bull bolted through, and Juliet saw immediately that he had blood on his face. He howled, and in answer, Crazy Horse cried out in the bathroom.

"Oh, baby," she sobbed, reaching for the big dog. He whined, and came over to her, and she could see he'd been cut, and blood was soaking into the fur above his eye, but the actual cut didn't seem dire.

"Come on. You, too." She opened the door to the bathroom, and Crazy Horse bolted out, running past her with a frantic, fierce bark, a charge she would never have expected from him, and he was out the dog door in three seconds.

"No!" she cried. "No! Crazy Horse! Wait!"

But he was gone, and the house was suddenly silent. She swallowed and stood still, peering into the yard. A break in the clouds allowed the faintest of moonlight to spill through, illuminating the shape of the dogs, and—maybe a coyote?

The animal cried out, the unmistakable, ragged, pained cry of a mountain lion. It gave a warning cry, low and long, and Juliet felt tears spring to her eyes, tears of fear, of empathy, of horror and a weird, sharp relief of understanding.

The dogs and the lion were intimately connected to her sister. Juliet desperately needed to do the right thing. What would Desi do right now?

The lion was desperately injured and in pain. It had been carrying a bullet around for days, and had to be half mad with pain by now. The dogs were only protecting their pack, the house, Juliet. They had to be her first priority—she couldn't let anything happen to them. Desi had lost enough.

She looked at the gun, remembering her sister's instructions about the safety, and she saw that it was on. She switched it off. Held the cold, heavy weight of it in her right hand. Her heart was pounding as she went to the door of the cabin and pulled it open the slightest bit.

The mountain lion bawled out a miserable cry, and she wished, desperately for another answer. "I don't want him to die," she said. "I hate this." Tears filled her eyes, her throat, her heart.

Juliet thought of her sister, tracking the poor beast all night long, tirelessly, all through the dark, snowy forest, cold, hungry, smarting, putting herself in danger to either save or put the animal out of pain. She pulled the door open and stepped on to the porch. The lion made a loud, agonizing sound, and she saw him on the ground, unmoving, as if he were dying.

The dogs howled, as if warning her or sending out a call to the other wolves, to the pack that no doubt paced restlessly in the runs at the sanctuary. They were so close to the dying mountain lion that she couldn't take a chance on firing from this distance.

It was dark. Her heart filled her throat, and tears ran down her face, making it hard to see well. She halted and steadied herself. It was important to forget herself and her fears right now, to act as Desi would act, to be selfless for the sake of the animals.

For *this* animal, who had no one else but her right now.

This wild, beautiful creature, stained and dirty with its travails the past few days lay on the ground, unable to move, and looked up at her. Its yellow eyes were full of misery, and Juliet almost felt as if the creature asked for release. She held up the gun, steadied her hand, and fired.

It lay still. Sitting Bull sat back on his haunches and lifted his nose to the sky, letting go of a long, singing howl. In the distance, the other wolves answered. Their cries rolled into the still night, as if to accompany the spirit of the mountain lion home, and Juliet, overcome, sank down beside the beautiful creature and wept.

And she would never tell a soul, but she swore she felt the animal's spirit move through her, in her chest and through her belly, velvety fur and fierce paws permeating her very cells, becoming one with her.

"Thank you," she breathed.

Sitting Bull and Crazy Horse, sensing her sorrow, came over and lapped her face. She stood up. "Come on, guys, let's go inside."

Josh drove up to the land an hour later, to see the lights were on inside, though he could see no sign of humans or dogs. It was the low, flickering light of a fire, and when he went inside, he found Juliet and the dogs lumped in a pile around the fire, all fast asleep.

He would have come sooner, frantic as he'd been with the sounds he'd heard over the phone, but it had taken some time to get hold of his mother, and he couldn't risk dragging Glory to a scene of mayhem.

But there was no mayhem. Relief, deep and wild, bolted through him, making his legs weak, and he sank onto a chair. One of the dogs had some blood on his face, and he could smell the lingering scent of overwrought wolf in the rooms, but for the rest, the scene was peaceful. Maybe he should go and let her sleep in peace.

Except—

She lay there so sweetly asleep in her nest of dogs and blankets, looking like the only thing he'd ever want again all his life. The soft tumble of her hair, shining in the reddish light, the curve of her shoulder, her pretty mouth. Voluptuous and wounded and strong and somehow innocent in spite of everything.

He fed the fire and took off his boots, then crept close and touched her arm. "Hey," he said quietly.

She opened her eyes. "Hi!" She blinked sleepily, peered at him with some confusion. "I told you everything was okay. You didn't have to come all the way up here."

"I know. I needed to make sure."

She blinked sleepily. "It was the lion," she said, drifting away.

"A lion?" He pictured the king of the beasts, roaring on the African veldt.

"Yes. I'll tell you about it in the morning." She shifted, pushing Tecumseh to one side. "Do you want to go to sleep with me?"

"Yes," Josh said, and took off his shoes and climbed in beside her. It was sudden and surprising and there were a thousand reasons not to fall in love, but it didn't appear he had a choice. He never wanted to sleep in a bed without her in it ever again.

When he settled beside her, she eased across the slight space between them and tucked her head into his shoulder. "Just right," she said. "Just right."

Chapter 16

In the morning, Juliet took Josh outside the back door to see the mountain lion. He squeezed her hand. "My mother is going to have some things to say about this."

"Did I do something wrong, do you think?"

"No way." He shook his head. "Let my mother talk to you. She's the medicine woman."

Juliet felt a sense of peace, looking that still body. In memory, she could hear the agonized cry, the wish for an end to pain. "Not sure what a person is supposed to do with such a thing." She looked up at him. "But it doesn't feel like an accident."

He made no comment, letting her find her own way through her thoughts.

"It was such a profound experience, and I'm not

sure what it all means yet, but I did figure out a lot last night, Josh."

"Like what?"

"I've been paralyzed by fear the past year, and I'm tired of it."

"It's normal, Juliet. People—"

She held up a hand. "Wait. I know it's normal to take some time to recover from a trauma. What's been hard for me was not the trauma itself, but the fact that I'm a good girl. I follow the rules. I did everything right and something terrible happened to me."

He nodded, listening. "Right."

"And now something terrible has happened to Desi, who doesn't deserve it, and—" She took a breath. "I just want to help her. Help other women like her, but I don't want to do it in a big, lonely city anymore. I'll find a way to serve women and the law here." She bit her lip. "I hope that's okay with you."

"It's very okay with me."

"I know it's soon, Josh, but I've fallen in love with you." She faced him, put his hand to her face. "It feels like I knew you before, that I've just been waiting for you."

He bent and hugged her, sighing. "Me, too," he said, and Juliet felt his voice through his chest, in her ear.

Juliet felt the losses and tensions and terrors of the past year suddenly flow out of her. Josh was home. "I love you," she said.

"I love you, too."

"How are we going to handle Glory?"

He chuckled. "I suspect she'll just handle us."

Juliet laughed. "I suspect you're right."

"Come on, let's get to town and report this, and go see Desi so she doesn't get too depressed."

Juliet nodded. She whistled for the dogs, and turned to find them sniffing something on the front step, a black shape. Tecumseh picked it up politely and carried it over to Juliet, depositing it at her feet with a happy grin. "Good dog," she said, automatically.

When she saw what it was, a blast of insight burned through the cobwebs in her brain. "Desi didn't kill Claude," she said. "The blood came from the altercation they had the other morning, remember?"

"Of course!"

She pointed to the dead raven at her feet. "And this is the third or fourth raven Desi has had on her porch. She thought it was Claude. Obviously it wasn't."

"We have to find out who it is."

Juliet nodded. "Yeah. We do."

Chapter 17

On Monday morning, Juliet drove her rental car down the muddy road to town to pick up her sister at the jail. The judge had set a $10,000 bond, secured by the land, and had apologized that he couldn't make it lower, but there was pressure on him from other sources, too. He also dismissed a request for an injunction by the now-deceased Claude Tsosie to force Desi to sell half the ranch.

Desi looked tired and pale when she emerged, but she came right to Juliet and hugged her hard. "I'm so proud of you!"

"For what?"

Desi laughed. "For the mountain lion. You did the right thing."

"Did I? I was so scared, Desi, but I was trying to think what you would do."

"Josh took the lion's body to Helene, and she's going to help you make a medicine bag if you like."

"A medicine bag?"

"She'll use some of the fur and the teeth and claws. The lion came to you, and you took care of her, and you have earned the right to call her your totem."

"My totem?" Juliet said in a whisper.

"Lion medicine," Desi said, brushing back her sister's hair. "You look like a lion, you know. You always have."

Juliet felt a press of emotions in her throat. She thought of the feeling of the lion moving through her, the breath of the creature in her lungs, and she promised herself she'd never speak of it. But it appeared she did not have to. "Thanks."

Desi punched her. "Pretty powerful totem, kiddo. I'm impressed."

"I didn't do anything, Desi. I tried to think what you would do."

"You were very brave, Juliet. You faced a situation that was way out of your league and handled it very well, with great compassion and empathy. The cat chose you. Don't dismiss it."

"No," she said, and it seemed she could feel the lion's heart within her. "No, I won't."

They walked into the bright day and Desi stopped on the sidewalk, and tipped her face up. "I wanted to die in there," she said quietly. "I can't go back. I *can't.*"

"I know." She took her hand. "We will not let it

happen. I promise." She smiled with her secret. "Come on, let's take a little walk up to Josh's house. Glory wants to tell you something."

"What?"

"You'll see."

The day was clear and busy, the sky arching like a turquoise balloon over the little town. As they passed the path that led to the shrine, a black-winged butterfly floated dizzily through the air. "Amazing how they live through the winter," Juliet said.

"The natural world is a great thing."

In quiet they walked up the street and down to Josh's house, where Glory waited on the porch in a fuzzy red coat, wearing a crown. "Desi!" she cried and flew off the porch into Desi's waiting arms. "I'm so happy you're out of jail!"

"Me, too, kiddo!" Desi kissed the little girl's cheek. "I hear you have something to tell me."

"I do! Where's my daddy?" Glory wiggled and Desi put her down.

Josh came out on the porch, and Juliet met his eyes, feeling as if the sun expanded to twelve times its size. He took his daughter's hand.

"Guess what?" Glory said.

"What?" Desi asked.

"My daddy is going to marry the princess!"

Desi shrieked. Literally, happily shrieked, then covered her mouth, and hugged Juliet so hard she thought her ribs would break. "Finally," she said, "a plan that worked out!"

"What plan?"

Desi laughed. "Never mind." She held out an arm to Josh and Glory. "Come on, let's have our first family hug!"

They embraced, Glory in the middle, Josh and Juliet side by side, Desi and Juliet hugging. Jack barked happily from the porch, then dived down the steps and slammed into Juliet's legs.

Juliet could not remember being happier and thought it was impossible to feel more until Josh leaned over and whispered in her ear, "I love you," and gently, sweetly, kissed her ear.

She raised her eyes. "Me, too."

* * * * *

A special treat for you from Harlequin Blaze!

Turn the page for a sneak preview of
DECADENT
by
New York Times *bestselling author*
Suzanne Forster

Available November 2006,
wherever series books are sold.

Harlequin Blaze—Your ultimate destination
for red-hot reads.
With six titles every month, you'll never guess
what you'll discover under the covers...

RUN, ALLY! Don't be fooled by him. He's evil. Don't let him touch you!

But as the forbidding figure came through the mists toward her, Ally knew she couldn't run. His features burned with dark malevolence, and his physical domination of everything around him seemed to hold her like a net.

She'd heard the tales. She knew all about the Wolverton legend and the ghost that haunted The Willows, an elegant old mansion lost by Micha Wolverton nearly a hundred years ago. According to folklore, the estate was stolen from the Wolvertons, and Micha was killed, trying to reclaim it. His dying vow was to be reunited with the spirit of his beloved wife, who'd taken her life for reasons no one would speak of, except in whispers. But Ally had never put much stock in the fantasy. She didn't believe in ghosts.

Until now—

She still didn't understand what was happening. The figure had materialized out of the mist that lay thick on the damp cemetery soil. A cool breeze and silvery moonlight had played against the ancient stone of the crypts surrounding her, until they joined the mist, causing his body to thicken and solidify right before her eyes. That was when she realized she'd seen this man before. Or thought she had, at least.

His face was familiar…so familiar, yet she couldn't put it together. Not with him looming so near. She stepped back as he approached.

"Don't be afraid," he said. His voice wasn't what she expected. It didn't sound as if it were coming from beyond the grave. It was deep and sensual. Commanding.

"Who are you?" she managed.

"You should know. You summoned me."

"No, I didn't." She had no idea what he was talking about. Two minutes ago, she'd been crouching behind a moss-covered crypt, spying on the mansion that had once been The Willows, but was now Club Casablanca. And then this—

If he was Micah, he might be angry that she was trespassing on his property. "I'll go," she said. "I won't come back. I promise."

"You're not going anywhere."

Words snagged in her throat. "Wh-why not? What do you want?"

"If I wanted something, Ally, I'd take it. This is about need."

His words resonated as he moved within inches of her. She tried to back away, but her feet were useless. "And you need something from me?"

"Good guess." His tone burned with irony. "I need lips, soft and surrendered, a body limp with desire."

"My lips, my bod—?"

"Only yours."

"Why? Why me?" This couldn't be Micha. He didn't want any woman but Rose. He'd died trying to get back to her.

"Because you want that, too," he said.

Wanted what? A ghost of her own? She'd always found the legend impossibly romantic, but how could he have known that? How could he know anything about her? Besides, she'd sworn off inappropriate men, and what could be more inappropriate than a ghost? She shook her head again, still not willing to admit the truth. But her heart wouldn't play along. It clattered inside her chest. The mere thought of his kiss, his touch, terrified her. This wildness, it was fear, wasn't it?

When his fingertips touched her cheek, she flinched, expecting his flesh to be cold, lifeless. It was anything but that. His skin was smooth and hot, gentle, yet demanding. And while his dark brown eyes were filled with mystery and wonder, there was a sensitivity about them that threatened to disarm her if she looked too deeply.

"These lips are mine," he said, as if stating a universal fact that she was helpless to avoid. In truth, it was just that. She couldn't stop him.

And she didn't want to.

* * * * *

Find out how the story unfolds in…
DECADENT
by
New York Times *bestselling author*
Suzanne Forster.
On sale November 2006.

Silhouette

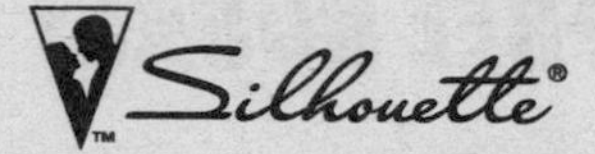

INTIMATE MOMENTS®

COMING NEXT MONTH

#1439 CLOSER ENCOUNTERS—Merline Lovelace
Code Name: Danger
Drew McDowell—Code name Riever—is curious to know why a recently fired defense attorney has developed a sudden interest in a mysterious WWII ship. When the mission takes a bizarre twist, the two must work together, while fighting an attraction that threatens to consume them both.

#1440 FULLY ENGAGED—Catherine Mann
Wingmen Warriors
Pararescueman Rick DeMassi never thought the woman he'd shared an incredible night with years ago would be his next mission. But when a stalker kidnaps her and his daughter, this air force warrior must face his greatest fears and save the two most important women in his life.

#1441 THE LOST PRINCE—Cindy Dees
Overthrown in a coup d'état, the future king of Baraq runs to the only woman who can help him. Now Red Cross aide Katy McMann must risk her life and her heart to help save a crumbling nation.

#1442 A SULTAN'S RANSOM—Loreth Anne White
Shadow Soldiers
To stop a biological plague from being released, mercenary Rafiq Zayed is forced to abduct Dr. Paige Sterling and persuade her to team up with him in a race against a deadly enemy…and their growing desires.

SIMCNM1006